MW00622431

Death and Doubloons

Nola Robertson

Copyright © 2019 Nola Robertson

Published by Nola Robertson, 2019

All rights reserved. No part of this publication may be reproduced, stored in a retrieval system, or transmitted, in any form or by any means, without the prior written permission of the author.

This is a work of fiction. Names, characters, places, and incidents are either the product of the author's imagination or are used fictitiously, and any resemblance to actual persons living or dead, business establishments, events, or locales, is entirely coincidental.

ISBN-13: 978-1-7328895-6-9

Also by Nola Robertson

Tarron Hunter Series

Hunter Bound
Hunter Enslaved
Hunter Unchained
Hunter Forbidden
Hunter Scorned
Hunter Avenged

Also Available

Stolen Surrender

St. Claire Witches

Hexed by Fire
Spelled With Charms

A Cumberpatch Cove Mystery

Death and Doubloons
Sabers, Sails, and Murder

CHAPTER ONE

Someone was going to commit murder, and I was pretty sure it would be me.

I stood in the doorway leading into the back office of Mysterious Baubles, the shop my family had owned for decades, and stared at the destruction on my desk. I'd only stepped away for five minutes, long enough to walk across the hall to the employee break room to retrieve some coffee before settling in to catch up on paperwork and enjoy my early morning breakfast.

I considered myself to be a patient person, not someone prone to losing their temper easily or committing any kind of violence. Today, however, I was going to make an exception. I'd been pushed to the limit of my endurance and was determined it make it him, rather than me, who'd be leaving the building permanently.

I carefully set my favorite porcelain cup filled with freshly brewed coffee on top of the nearest filing cabinet and braced my hands on my hips, then met my opponent's dark, beady glare with one of my own. This wasn't the first time this week I'd pondered creative ways to execute my plans for the creature's demise. And being a five-foot, five-inch woman weighing one hundred and ten pounds, possibly one hundred and thirteen—no scale available to confirm or deny—I was fairly confident I could take the small, gray, and furry four-legged creature with little pink feet and a hairless pink tail.

Whiskers twitching, he rose on his hind legs, utterly unimpressed and undaunted by my presence. Caught in the grasp of his clawed clutches was a morsel of the delectable cream cheese muffin I'd purchased from Mattie's Coffee Shop across the street.

A quick glance at the crumbs lining the plate and the gaping hole in the no longer edible dome-shaped cake only irritated me more. When my muffin-stealing nemesis had the audacity to make a production out of stuffing another tasty crumb into his mouth, I lost it.

Growling wasn't something I normally did either, but I was making noises like a rabid dog at the gray furball who'd cost me two out of three of my favorite morning meals. Since I lived alone and my cooking skills lacked the aptitude of anything closely resembling those of a decent chef, I either prepared something that came out of a box or visited one of the few food serving establishments within walking distance of my small yet comfortable apartment.

The nearest thing within reach happened to be a paperweight, one of many similar touristy items sold in the shops throughout the town. Encased inside the round half globe of clear, hard plastic was a miniature pirate's ship and the words "Cumberpatch Cove, Maine" scrawled in a beautiful neon blue script beneath it.

Knowing I wasn't athletically inclined didn't stop me from cocking my arm like a professional baseball player and tossing the oval dome. Of course, it missed its target, did a double bounce across the desktop, scattering all the neatly stacked papers in its wake before slamming into the bordering wall with a loud thump.

If mice could smile, this one was practically sneering with triumph. In a flash of fur, he scurried across the surface, shuffling the papers even more before sailing off the edge. He made a graceful landing on the seat of my chair, then continued his descent until he reached the floor and disappeared under the desk.

The building was old and constantly in need of minor repairs. I wasn't sure how he continually accessed my office, but it was a good guess he'd found a crack somewhere in the floorboard along the wall, and I was determined to keep him from escaping.

"Oh, no you don't."

Needing something to capture the arrogant little varmint, I grabbed the plastic trash can off the floor, which thankfully only contained some crumpled papers I'd tossed inside the day before. I hastily emptied the contents onto the floor, then shoved the chair out of the way, dropped on my hands and knees, and crawled under the desk.

It didn't take long to find him. Instead of scampering off, he stood on all fours facing me, his gaze focused as if studying a chess opponent. Turning the can upside down, I held my breath and slowly eased it toward him.

Hasty footsteps creaked on the old hardwood floor, then abruptly stopped in the doorway. "Rylee, are you okay?" Abigail Spencer, Abby to her friends, Grams to me, continued in a concerned voice. "It sounded like this half of the building collapsed." I could see the rounded tips of her brown leather pumps peeking out beneath the hem of a dark blue pleated skirt. "Are we having an earthquake? Is that why you're hiding under the desk?" She pushed the chair aside. "In all the years I've lived here, I don't recall us ever having a single one. But I suppose there's always a first time."

I loved my grandmother, knew she meant well, but at the moment, I could do without her gift for exaggerating a situation. I rolled my eyes at my newly inherited business partner. My parents, Caroline and Jonathan Spencer, were the true shop owners and, after announcing their retirement plans included travel, had informed me that I would be left in charge of running the place.

Actually, it was my mother who wanted to travel. My father only went along because it kept her happy and gave him a chance to do what he loved best—search the world outside our small coastal town for anything to prove his theories about magic were correct. Witchcraft, hauntings, the undead, anything that couldn't be reasonably explained or verified with images and articles on the Internet, qualified.

I suppose when you lived in a community where more than half the inhabitants were obsessed with the supernatural, it was hard not to become an enthusiast. I, on the other hand, didn't have the same belief, had never witnessed anything otherworldly, and consistently voiced my skepticism about the topic.

I lowered the can with a frustrated sigh. "I'm fine, Grams." I wasn't fine, definitely wouldn't be fine until I'd captured the furry muffin-stealing thief who'd taken advantage of the interruption to scurry across the wooden floor and disappear into the gap behind the lateral filing cabinet. "No earthquake."

"Then what are you doing under there?"

"Nothing." Embarrassed, I shifted when her gaze locked on to the overturned wastebasket.

With a swish of polyester, Grams got to her feet. "I hope your 'nothing' means you weren't trying to catch Howard."

Dread crept along my spine as I crawled backward and asked, "Who is Howard?" I misjudged the distance to the underside of the desk and banged my head. "Ouch." I winced, rubbing my hand over the sore spot on the back of my skull as I used the edge to pull myself up from the floor.

Grams shook her head so her straight dark chocolate strands peppered with silver bounced against her jawline. She pressed her multi-ringed hands to her hips and scolded me with dark cinnamon eyes. "He's the mouse who's been living in the shop for the past few weeks." The exasperation in her tone sounded as if Howard's status was common knowledge and how dare I not be aware of it.

"Why did you name the mouse?" Years of knowing better didn't stop my mouth from operating before thinking about the ramifications of my verbal slip. Maybe the thump to my head had caused brain damage. Asking my grandmother why an animal, any animal, had a name gained me the same scowl I received every time I discussed my doubts about the existence of ghosts with anyone living in our coastal community. The existence, or nonexistence in my case, of one ghost in particular—Martin Cumberpatch. The notoriously infamous pirate Cumberpatch Cove had been named after was rumored to haunt our town, searching for his buried treasure.

The town's main source of revenue was derived from tourists, many of whom came here hoping to get a glimpse of the pirate's ghost or any spirit rumored to be haunting our local cemetery. Personally, I was a need-to-see-it-with-my-own-eyes kind of gal and didn't believe the stories I'd been forced to listen to since childhood. Besides contending with my family's eccentricities, I was also burdened with the responsibility of ensuring the shop made a profit, which meant I had to set aside my nonbeliefs. At least around our customers.

Grams tsked and waggled her finger at me. "Howard is special, and you know very well I didn't name him. He is your great-great uncle on my side of the family."

Uh-oh. A familiar tightness gripped my chest. According to Grams, our departed relatives spoke to her in dreams, giving her brief glimpses of their so-called quests. Personally, I thought it had something to do with the occasional shot of whiskey she had before going to bed, but that was just me. I also didn't believe there was a swinging door to the spirit world, but Grams was convinced that under dire circumstances, spirits were allowed to return and help family members.

I knew arguing with Grams about her reincarnation visions would be worse than crossing a minefield without a metal detector. But if I had to suffer through more muffin-stealing episodes, I deserved to know why. "If the mouse *really* is my great-great uncle, then what is he doing here?"

For some reason, this particular uncle had been nominated as my family's champion, because I could recall two other times he'd been mentioned in otherworldly visits. The first time, Howard had appeared as a neighbor's dog when I was ten, and his second visit was as a cousin's pet hamster. The hamster had an issue with its bladder every time I set him in my lap and hadn't reassured me that his supposed possession by my deceased relative was a good thing.

And, from what I remembered, neither visit preceded or prevented a monumental disaster, though I wasn't about to point that fact out to Grams.

"You know my dreams aren't always clear, but I believe he is here to help *you*." Grams sounded convinced.

"Me, why?" I couldn't imagine anything I needed help with. Other than running the shop and keeping Grams out of trouble, a full-time job by itself, I didn't have much time for anything else.

Before she could give me an answer, the faint tinkling of a bell echoed from the hallway. It signaled someone's arrival and the end to our conversation.

"I'll take care of the customer"—Grams frowned at the disarray on my desk and the contents from the trash can scattered on the floor— "while you clean up this mess. And don't do anything else to upset Howard." She cast one more admonishing glare in my direction, then, with a twirl of her skirt, left the room.

All I could do was shake my head and survey the damage. The untouched coffee was cold, the muffin inedible, and the top of the desk, which usually had some semblance of organization, was in shambles. I picked up the paperweight, noting the new crack running along one side of the plastic dome, and cringed.

Logically, I knew it was a contradiction in beliefs to be superstitious about marring the smooth surface when I was skeptical about the supernatural. Just to make sure I had nothing to worry about and hadn't inadvertently earned myself several years of bad luck, I planned to check one of the many handbooks on the subject shelved in the far corner of the shop.

I returned the dome to its designated spot on the bookshelf with the rest of the odd souvenirs I'd collected during the occasional family vacation throughout the years. Afterward, I refilled the trash can and organized my desktop, silently cursing Howard the entire time.

It was a long-standing rule that Spencers did not, under any circumstances, harm another member of the family, even if the member was already dead. Now that the mouse held an honorary spot under my grandmother's watchful eye, my plan to set out traps later today was no longer going to happen.

Even though I didn't believe the mouse was a reincarnated relative, it didn't mean I would purposely do anything to hurt Grams's feelings. No matter how outrageous or misguided they might be.

CHAPTER TWO

While I'd been picking up trash and reorganizing paperwork after my battle with Howard, the bell had tinkled several more times. I didn't think there was a single store or business on Swashbuckler Boulevard, the town's main street, that didn't have a similar old-fashioned bell hanging over their doorways. I walked into the shop, taking a quick survey of the customers milling around and perusing our collection of unique and, what I considered to be an odd, selection of items.

The store had a little bit of everything. There were glass cases containing unusual jewelry, some with supposed magical value. We had shelves stocked with herbal remedies, scented candles, and tarot cards. We even had a section dedicated to pirate lore, including eye patches, stuffed talking parrots, toy cutlasses, and swords.

I spotted Grams on the other side of the room engaged in a conversation with a middle-aged woman wearing a bright green T-shirt emblazoned with a pirate ship logo and an oversized bag draped over her shoulder. My grandmother might be pushing seventy, but she had the sharp wit of a twenty-year-old, rarely missed a thing, and handled the role of sweet, attentive clerk with an admirable, if not somewhat misleading, finesse.

I hadn't missed the tight smile and reproachful roll of her eyes currently aimed in my direction. Okay, so it might take Grams a little longer than I'd thought for her to get over my attempt to return our so-called, yet-to-be-proved, long-deceased relative to his home in the spirit plane.

I stepped behind the counter where we kept the cash register and saw Jade's golden-brown leather purse, an imitation of a famous brand I could never remember, sitting on the shelf under the counter. She was a full-time employee, one of my two best friends in the world, and my complete opposite. She was into fashion, primping, and polished nails. I was more comfortable in a pair of worn jeans and a baggy T-shirt. Not that I didn't own a decent dress or two, along with a few pairs of nice pants. Being the acting manager meant being in charge. It also meant I had to look professional, or at least professionalish when I came to work.

Jade must have been running late before she arrived, because she normally made a point of stopping by the office for a visit before starting her shift.

I pushed worrying about appeasing Grams out of my mind and focused on the appointment I had with Jessica Jenkins. She was due to arrive any minute, and I needed Jade's help locating her order.

No matter how much I stressed the importance of using the back storeroom for additional items or special customer orders, things had a tendency of relocating to unusual places. Places I would never think to look.

The interior of the shop was like a maze. Even though the majority of the center-aisle shelves and displays were much taller than me, Jade was easy to find. All I had to do was follow the humming. A vocalist my friend wasn't, and I'd been glad my mother had nixed my father's suggestion to install a music system into the shop when I was still in my teens.

There'd been too many days in my past that I'd spent

avoiding unwanted attention, mostly because my younger self didn't rank high on any popularity list. Something I was sure was related to the craziness of my family.

My goal to remain invisible to anyone other than my close friends was made worse by Jade's obsessive need to break out into a lyrical rendition—more of a crackly squawk—to whatever song was playing wherever we went.

I turned left and headed down an aisle I'd appropriately dubbed dark and ominous because the shelves were lined with everything a paranormal enthusiast coveted. I followed that with a quick right and found her kneeling on the floor facing away from me. She was busily stocking a lower shelf with herbal remedies, my insistent mother's contribution to the wide variety of items we sold.

I quashed the impulse to jump-start Jade's morning by sneaking up on her. Actually, I was more afraid of having something tossed at my head. She used to play softball and had a good throwing arm. I ought to know. I'd worn a welt on my forehead for nearly a week from the last time she'd been spooked and tossed a candle at me.

"Morning," I said in combination with weighting my footsteps to make the wooden floor creak and announce my arrival.

"Hey, Rylee," Jade said cheerily as she glanced over her shoulder. She got to her feet and smoothed out her black cotton skirt before fluffing the ruffled hem hitting the middle of her thighs. She slipped her bare feet into a pair of two-inch open-toed teal heels sitting next to her on the floor, boosting her slim height even higher.

I couldn't ever remember a time when my friend wasn't obsessed with footwear. The higher the heel, the better. An obsession I could never understand. She was always prodding me to change my mundane fashion and invest in a pair of shiny pumps, using my shorter height and the possibility of attracting a man's attention as a motivator.

I had two problems with her enthusiastic need to help me improve my appearance and my wardrobe. One, I believed in comfort first. There was no way I could maintain my balance on wedged platforms sitting higher than a half inch off the ground, let alone walk on them. I'd fallen off enough stepladders to prove my theory was correct. And two, I had no interest in dating a guy who was more interested in staring at my ankles than paying attention to my face.

Jade checked to see if anyone was standing nearby, then cleared her throat through a giggle. "I heard you tried to take out one of your great-great uncles...Harvey? Harold?"

"Howard, and don't start." Having to deal with my family's eccentricities was bad enough. I didn't need my friend rubbing it in or encouraging my grandmother's crazy reincarnation notions.

"Wouldn't think of it."

Jade's grin said otherwise, but I let it go. "Jessica's supposed to be here any minute. You wouldn't by any chance know where those boxes with the treasure chests ended up, would you?"

"They're in the storeroom."

Figuring it would be a waste of time, I hadn't bothered to stop and check the room when I left my office. "Seriously, where are they?" I scoffed, since anyone putting something where it belonged would be the first in a history of firsts.

"Third shelf on the left. Do you want me to get them for you?" Jade chided with a wink.

"No, I'll do it." I sidestepped the three plastic bottles sitting on the floor and headed for the storeroom. I was shocked and relieved to find the boxes shelved exactly where Jade said they'd be. I had just finished loading the handcart and wheeling it toward the front of the shop when I heard Jessica's voice and her enthusiastic "Good morning."

"Be right there," I hollered and leaned the cart, along with the three stacked boxes, against the wall in the hallway. After grabbing the top box, I headed back into the shop.

The yearly Founders Day weekend was a big event for our town. Jessica had spent a lot of time and effort convincing the committee to sponsor her idea to have a yearly treasure hunt in the local cemetery. Once the members of the committee learned I had a lot of experience in dealing with online vendors—thanks to Jade—I'd been volunteered without consent to be in charge of ordering the yearly prizes. I hadn't complained too loudly because Greg Abernathy, owner of the Cumberpatch Cove Pirate Museum, had been impressed with my skills and hired me, via my family's shop, to supply the pirate museum with miniature toy chests filled with chocolates wrapped in gold foil for his visitors. I was sure he'd meant them to be giveaways for children, but I'd seen numerous adults carrying them around and enjoying their delectable contents.

"I hope these will work." I knew being successful meant a great deal to Jessica, and I didn't want to let her down. After setting the cardboard container on the counter, I peeled back the flaps.

Jessica tucked her chin-length hair behind her ears. "Judging by the pictures you sent me, I'm sure they'll be great." She stood an inch or so taller than me, so peering inside the box without standing on her tiptoes wasn't a problem.

The contents had been packed in three neat rows stacked on top of one another with each chest individually protected by a sheet of thin Bubble Wrap. I slipped one of the chests out of the package I'd opened previously and handed it to her. The box was a miniature replica of a pirate's chest with a stained wooden finish, the lid and corners edged with golden trim. Each one was filled with fake coins stamped with a design replicating a doubloon.

Martin Cumberpatch's popularity might not come close to that of well-known names such as Blackbeard and

William Kidd, but I thought having a treasure hunt seemed a fitting way to honor the town's founder. For those of us who didn't sleep through Mr. Blackthorne's boring history class, we'd learned Martin's notoriety was a bit sketchy. Other than the rumor that he'd buried his stolen treasure somewhere within or near the confines of our town, there wasn't much information available about our founding figure.

Somehow, the lack of anything tangible didn't stop the yearly influx of tourists from pouring into Cumberpatch and supporting the local vendors, my family's shop included. Heck, just last year, we even had a tour bus add our not so quaint little village to their coastal travel route.

"Rylee, these are perfect." Jessica held up the box, twisting it in different directions for a closer examination.

"Thanks." I smiled proudly, not above accepting praise for my hard work. I'd spent several hours searching the Internet before I found a site I liked that specialized in all things related to pirates. I'd been so impressed by their wide selection and reasonable prices that I'd saved the online store as a bookmark on my computer. I intended to revisit the website later and purchase some items for the shop to sell during the annual Cumberpatch pirate festival in the fall.

Another tinkling of the bell reminded me that we were going to have a busy day. Unfortunately, our newest visitor was Lavender Abbott, committee co-chair and the biggest pain in my backside since grade school. I stopped myself before I groaned loud enough to be heard, then mentally calculated whether or not I could make it to the hall leading to the back of the building before she saw me. My odds for escape were good, but what kind of person would I be if I abandoned poor Jessica to the town's obnoxious harpy?

As the person in charge of the group's most prominent event in years, Jessica had replaced me in the number one spot on Lavender's list of those she despised. A position continually rewarded with Lavender's negative focus and an itemized list of personal shortcomings.

I sucked in the less than endearing words preparing to blast from my mouth and said, "Good morning, Lavender."

I received a disdainful smirk for my polite efforts, followed by a grimace as she perused the surrounding shelves. "Looking for something specific?" I scrounged to add a drop of sweetness to my voice, knowing that Lavender had never, and would never, purchase anything from my family's store.

Finished stocking the last of the herbal remedies, Jade appeared behind Lavender, carrying an empty box. She quirked a brow in my direction, a silent inquiry asking me why I would purposely prod the viper.

Old habits, I guess. I answered her quirk with a shrug. Our shop might be popular with the tourists, but Lavender wouldn't waste her time coming inside, not without having a spectacularly good reason. Or bad in my case, since every visit came with condescending comments and a certain need to cause trouble. Her snarky comments I could tolerate, and had for years. It was the "trouble" part of her visit I anxiously hoped to avoid.

"As if," she snorted, heading straight for Jessica and the open box of chests.

I bit back a sharp reply and ground my teeth so hard, I was certain I'd cracked something and would be making an appointment to see my dentist by the end of the week.

"The only reason I'm here is because Serena asked me to remind everyone about the meeting tonight," Lavender said with her usual condescending zeal.

Personally, I'd have been happy to receive a phone call. A text would have been even better. Serena was Lavender's older sister, and only slightly more reasonable to deal with. She could be a bit of a snob, but of the two, she was nicer, though not by much. Serena was also in charge of the Founders Day committee. And like it or not, all the shop owners whose business resided on Swashbuckler Boulevard were required to participate. It seemed darned inconvenient that my parents always managed to leave on one trip or another several days before the first meeting, which always left attending up to Grams and me.

Lavender scowled at Jessica. "She'll also expect you to give everyone an update on your progress."

"Glad to." Jessica's sugary-sweet imitation sounded more practiced than mine. She shared a dramatic eye roll with Jade and me as soon as Lavender wasn't looking.

Jade covered her mouth, because if she coughed any harder, something besides a stifled laugh was going to come out.

"Are these the chests?" Lavender sneered and poked at the ornate box sitting on the counter. "It's not as nice as I'd hoped, but I guess it will have to do."

I refused to be baited. Grams, on the other hand, had no qualms about coming to the aid of her beloved granddaughter. She'd finished helping her customers and was now standing next to Jade, glaring at Lavender. "You'll have to admit the treasure hunt is a lot more fun than those silly old tea parties Elsa used to have at the inn."

Though there'd been a lot of speculation, no one in my family knew the real reason the Abbotts and the Spencers didn't get along. Whatever it was had been monumental, something that happened between Lavender's grandmother Elsa and Grams years ago. Something rumored to involve my late grandfather. And whatever *it* was had earned me a spot on the top of Lavender's dislike list without me even trying.

Lavender gasped. Her jaw moved but no words came out. Another first for today. Once she recovered her shock, her angry gaze sparked with determination, and I braced for a nasty comeback. Luckily, Shawna, the other member of my best friend trio, picked that moment to walk into the shop.

"Morning, all." Shawna sauntered toward our group, her smile beaming, her sneakers squeaking on the hardwood floor. She ignored Lavender's frown and flushed cheeks and asked, "Hey, are you still hosting the meeting tonight?"

Shawna had added several bright purple streaks to her unruly light brown hair since the last time I'd seen her. Her outfit, a black skirt and cobalt-blue T-shirt, was the standard uniform for the Cumberpatch Cove Cantina. Stamped on the left side of her shirt was a logo bearing a pirate ship with the restaurant's name printed across the center of it. Most days, she covered the lunch-hour shift and made a point of stopping by the shop on her way to work.

"Of course. It will be in the usual room at the inn." A hint of a smile spread across Lavender's lips.

I'd never been able to figure out why Shawna was the only one in my small circle of friends who Lavender tolerated.

"Great. Can't wait." Shawna slapped the newspaper she had tucked under her arm on the counter.

Lavender gripped the strap of her expensive leather purse and headed for the door. "Now if you'll excuse me, I'm busy and have more people to remind about the meeting."

"Could have used the phone," Grams muttered as she moved to take the spot Lavender had vacated. "Impertinent wench...just like her grandmother."

"How so?" I innocently asked, hoping Grams might finally reveal some information about the taboo secret from her past.

The wrinkles deepened around her narrowed gaze. "Never you mind."

I wasn't offended when Shawna pushed the box out of the way and didn't comment on the treasure chest. I'd learned long ago that nothing came between her and the daily ritual of reading the newspaper. After taking over the counter and less than a minute of reading, she tapped a black-and-white photo on the first page. "This...this is terrible."

"What's terrible?" Jade set the empty box on the floor and walked around the long counter to stand next to me.

Even Jessica and Grams crowded in closer to see what Shawna was pointing at.

I wasn't great at reading upside down, but I didn't have a problem making out the bold print in the headline's article: LOCAL MAN SLAIN DURING DOUBLOON HEIST.

"You remember Lyle Crumpet, don't you?" Shawna asked. "He works at the pirate museum."

Jade snapped her fingers. "Isn't he the guy who gave us tours when our history class went there on field trips?"

"Yep, that's him," Shawna said.

Jessica, who'd moved to town only a few years ago, also nodded in agreement. I didn't think there was anyone who lived in Cumberpatch that hadn't visited the museum and taken at least one of Lyle's tours.

A tight pain clamped my chest. "What happened?" I hoped the connection I'd made between Lyle and the article's mention of someone's death weren't true. "Is he...is he...dead?" I had fond memories of the kindly old man. He was an excellent guide with a gift for making tales about the past seem magical. He'd worked at the museum most of his life and no doubt would have worked there until he retired.

I remembered running into him a few weeks ago. His son's wife had recently had a baby. The twenty-plus pictures he showed me on his phone were proof he was enjoying the time he spent with his new granddaughter.

"According to this, Lyle's body was found in the Bangor museum after closing two days ago," Shawna said.

"I wonder why it took so long to make the headlines?" Jade asked.

"I'll bet they didn't want to release the information until they had a chance to contact his family," Grams said.

Besides the local history class trips, I'd also visited the museum in Bangor a few times with my parents. The place had an extensive collection of pirate artifacts, including some well-preserved doubloons obtained from a sunken ship somewhere off our coastline.

Shawna moved her finger as she continued to read. "Apparently, some rare doubloons were stolen, and the city police are speculating that Lyle was somehow involved in the robbery."

I frowned, tucking my arms firmly across my chest. "No way." I'd known Lyle for years, not in a close, we-were-personal-friends-and-met-to-do-things-once-a-week sort of way, but more of a stop-and-chat-whenever-we-passed-each-other-on-the-street kind of way. I couldn't believe he was capable of committing such an awful crime, or any crime, for that matter.

As far as I knew, he didn't have any friends or family living in Bangor. If he did go there to visit the museum, what was he doing in the place after it closed? And more importantly, how had he gotten inside if it was locked?

Lyle being blamed for the robbery didn't make any sense and bothered me more than a little. Later, when I had time and was alone, I planned to read the newspaper article, then maybe do some online research.

"You've been to that museum a few times. Any idea what happened?" Grams asked, staring expectantly at me. Her question had Jade, Shawna, and Jessica doing the same.

"How should I know?" Being a professed psychic was my grandmother's thing, not mine. So I wasn't sure why she assumed a few visits to a museum qualified me as an expert, not when the topic involved theft and murder.

The bell tinkled, the door opened, and a woman entered the shop dragging a small girl of maybe six or seven behind her. It was a welcome interruption, and I released a sigh when Grams hurried from the group to greet them.

Jessica was the first one to break up the silent pondering of Lyle's death. "I don't want to be late for my morning tour, so I should get going. Afterward, I'll start hiding the chests."

Jessica worked as a guide at the By the Bay cemetery. Because the graveyard was the resting spot of our town's famous pirate, it had gained a lot of notoriety over the years. The constant rumors that the place was haunted only added to the influx of tourists and visiting spirit enthusiasts. Personally, I found the place a little creepy, even during the daylight hours.

"Oh, and here." Jessica picked up the unwrapped chest and handed it to me. "This is for doing such a great job. But you have to promise me you won't tell Lavender."

"Might be kind of hard to do…" I winked and secured the flaps on the cardboard box. "Since we're such besties and all."

Jessica giggled. "That makes two of us."

"If you need any help hiding the chests, let me know," Jade said.

"Me too," Shawna added.

"You know if she lets you help, then you won't be able to participate in the hunt," I said.

"Rylee's right. You'd be disqualified and miss out on all the fun," Jessica said.

Since I was the one who ended up carrying the spade, doing the digging, then letting Jade and Shawna claim the prizes, then yeah, I was okay with missing out on the fun.

"Let me get the rest of the chests and I'll help you take them out to your car." I picked up the box and went to retrieve the handcart where I'd left it in the hallway.

CHAPTER THREE

I concentrated on helping Jessica get the boxes into her car and ignored the rumbling noises my stomach made every time someone opened the door to Mattie's shop and the smell of freshly baked goodies wafted out to the sidewalk.

Even if someone invented steroids for cars, no amount of muscle-building would improve the size of Jessica's eight-year-old two-door coupe. Or increase the size of her tiny trunk.

With the help of some red-and-green Christmas ribbon she had stashed underneath the front seat, we were able to secure the boxes inside. It was May, long past the holiday season. It might seem strange for someone to keep colorful ribbon stored in their car, but since strange was a normal part of my life, I didn't bother asking.

"Thanks again." She opened the driver's-side door and tossed her purse onto the passenger seat.

"No problem. I'll see you tonight." I hung around long enough to watch her do a pretzel imitation to get inside, then rolled the cart to the crosswalk. Instead of having to wait for the light to stop traffic, I'd arrived at the same moment the pedestrian signal flashed, announcing it was safe to cross the street.

When I reached the sidewalk on the other side, I turned to give Jessica a final wave. I glimpsed a man slipping from the shadows of the alley that separated Mattie's building from the one next to it. He was tall and wore faded jeans and a lightweight navy-blue jacket. Pretty much the usual attire for anyone out walking during the chilly morning hours.

He wasn't anyone I recognized, and from this angle, I couldn't get a good look at his face. If he hadn't nervously been tugging on the hood and trying to keep his features hidden, I might have ignored him and gone inside. Instead, I found it disturbing and continued to watch what he was doing.

He walked over to Jessica's vehicle and knocked on her window. She must have known the guy, because she got out of her car and started to speak with him. I wasn't an expert on body language, but by the way she tucked her hair behind her ear, then crossed her arms, I'd say she was more frustrated than angry.

Just in case I'd misread the situation, I was ready to cross the street and offer some noninterfering, mostly nosy assistance. I'd propped the handcart against the building and made it two steps when I heard "Mornin', Rylee."

I recognized the overly friendly voice of Al Jacobs, the local package delivery person. He had the worst timing and was the biggest gossip. Ignoring him wasn't a good idea, nor was letting him take an interest in what was happening with Jessica. "Hey, Al," I greeted him cheerily, then shifted sideways so I could watch Jessica and keep Al focused on me. As he was six foot three, seeing his face was like trying to view the highest branches in a tree. I tipped my head back and used my hand to block out the sun. "How's it going?"

"Oh, you know, same old stuff. Got a package here from your dad." He retrieved the box he'd tucked between his beefy arm and his chest. I wasn't his first customer of the day, evidenced by the patch of sweat seeping near the underarm of his shirt and the metallic smell clinging to his body. He adjusted the waistband of his dark tan pants, but no amount of tugging was going to move them above the paunch of his belly.

"Suppose it's something interesting for the shop." He inquisitive focus never left the package.

My father's fascination with the paranormal was well-known throughout Cumberpatch, hence Al's interest in the box's contents.

I shrugged. "Who knows?" I wasn't going to open the box no matter how much he stared at it, and hoped my disinterest would lead the conversation in a different direction. "Need a signature?" I wiggled my fingers and noted that the guy was still talking to Jessica.

"Sure do." Al grinned and unclipped the small electronic device attached to his belt. "Hey, if you're not busy Friday night, you should stop by the saloon. With all the extra tourists in town for the celebration, the bar is going to be packed this weekend."

At thirty-five, Al was the oldest member of a local band that played most weekends at the Shivering Timbers Saloon, the most popular bar in Cumberpatch. He was a decent drummer with an unfulfilled dream of hitting it big, which was probably why the length of his dark brown hair never got shorter than his shoulders. While he was working, he kept his hair fastened with a tie at his nape and had removed the fancy stud earring he assured me guaranteed him the attention of the local female population.

"I'll have to see how things go with the treasure hunt first." I enjoyed listening to music and dancing as much as the next person, but pushing my way through an overcrowded room wasn't my idea of a good time.

Al tapped the device's tiny screen several times with his digital pen before handing both of them to me. "Your grandmother mentioned you were helping out with the committee this year. How's that going?"

"Fine. How about you, are you signing up for the treasure hunt?" I asked more out of politeness than anything else.

I glanced in Jessica's direction again and was relieved to see she was back in her car and pulling away from the curb. The guy she'd been conversing with had his hands tucked in his front pockets and was solemnly skulking down the sidewalk in the opposite direction.

"Yep, wouldn't miss it." Al returned the device to his belt. "I guess I'll see you there."

"Guess so," I said, turning to grab my cart and head into the shop.

The woman and the child Grams had been assisting when I left were gone, and she was helping a new customer in the magical relic section. The items weren't the ancient treasures the overhead sign depicted, and unless having the ability to zap, glow, or make eerie noises qualified as enchanted, they weren't magical either. Though none of that seemed to matter to the paranormal enthusiasts who visited our town.

Shawna and Jade were hovering, heads together, next to the display case. The newspaper was still spread out on the counter, but, if I had to guess, was now open to the astrology page. For as long as I'd known Shawna, she never missed reading her daily forecast. She also made sure the rest of us knew what the cosmic universe had planned for our day. I didn't need anyone telling me how my stars lined up to know I was going to be enjoying the chocolates my mother sent me. When I'd spoken to her a few days ago, she'd told me to expect a delivery of some delicious imported sweets.

I tucked the cart in an out-of-the-way corner with the intention of returning it to the storage room later. Fortunately, one glance at the newspaper told me that Shawna had moved on to another section and I'd missed out on hearing forecasts. I relaxed and set the package on the end of the counter.

"What's in the box?" Shawna gave it a brief glance, then went back to reading.

Unless there were gossipy tidbits involved, Shawna had a tendency to slip in and out of conversations on a regular basis. I protectively patted the cardboard, uninterested in sharing the contents with my friends. "Oh, nothing important."

CHAPTER FOUR

Shortly after Shawna left for her shift, the shop filled up with more customers. Enough to keep all of us busy working non-stop for the rest of the morning. With Grams agreeing to handle customers while Jade popped down to the cantina, I was finally able to squeeze in a break shortly before noon. Since I'd lost my breakfast to Howard, I was starving and couldn't wait for Jade to get back with our lunch.

Thinking about food reminded me that I hadn't opened the package from my mother or checked out the delectable sweets inside. What could one chocolate hurt? It wasn't as if it was going to ruin my appetite or add additional weight to my already rounded hips and backside. I snagged the box along with the chest Jessica had given me and headed for the office.

I'd been so distracted thinking about the guy who'd stopped Jessica that I hadn't paid any attention to the addresses listed on the box. The label was clearly addressed to me, but had Madame Minerva's Magical Wonders listed as the sender. The physical address listed on the box was in Florida, so I assumed my mother had been shopping with my father when she'd found the imported delicacies she'd mentioned during her last call.

I'd never heard of Madame Minerva's before and thought it was a strange name for a business that sold candy. If the chocolates were as good as my mother promised, then who was I to judge?

My parents were taking their first Caribbean cruise and had left a few days early to play tourist in the southern coastal states before their ship was scheduled to sail. My father had been excited when he showed me his itinerary of the places he'd slated to visit. Some regular shopping to appease my mother, a couple of shops that specialized in paranormal paraphernalia, and at least five haunted locations documented to have actual spirit sightings.

Besides my father, who'd usually made me accompany him rather than allow me to shop with my mother, I was probably the person in Cumberpatch who'd clocked in the most hours visiting haunted sights during family vacations. Other than some creaking floors or a few unexplained door slams, neither of us had ever seen an actual ghost. For that, I'd been thankful.

Anxious to see what was in the box, I grabbed a pair of scissors out of the pencil holder near my computer. I sliced a thin line along the seam of the tape securing the flaps of the lid together. Inside the box, amongst a pile of Styrofoam peanuts, was a plastic case with a rounded lid. The glossy cerulean-blue surface was randomly decorated with miniature silver stars, the edges painted with gold curlicues, and reminded me of a child's glittery jewelry box.

When I popped the small clasp on the side, I figured I'd been sent the wrong order and expected to find the case filled with beads and small bottles of brightly colored fingernail polishes. Instead, there was a long, red velvet bag embroidered with more miniature stars and a filigree braid wrapped around the fabric on one end. What caught my attention and interested me the most was the inscription painted in bold black script on the underside of the lid.

Be warned thee who seeks to invoke those of the otherworldly realm.

The gift of the spirit seeker bears great responsibility and should not be taken lightly.

I had no idea what the heck a spirit seeker was, or why the manufacturer thought they needed to include an ominous warning to their creative gimmick. I was intrigued after finding the decorative bag inside the case. I was so impressed that I gave myself a mental reminder to thank my mother later for finding such a unique gift, then see about ordering some of them for the shop.

I picked up the bag, impatient to see what the contents looked like. It was heavier than I imagined and appeared to be solid, making me think it was a single bar of candy. Once I removed the string, I tipped the bag and was disappointed when a long cylinder of dark wood spilled into my hand.

Approximately two inches in diameter, the cylinder was etched with ornate swirling patterns. The craftsmanship was so beautiful, I couldn't resist picking it up for a closer look. I laid it across my palm, then ran a fingertip along the polished surface, awed by the unusual carvings, yet surprised by the wood's extremely cold temperature.

After a single stroke, the symbols began to glow a shimmering crystal blue and the surface gradually warmed. "What the..." It reminded me of a heat pack, the way the plastic warms after snapping the activator inside. Only I hadn't snapped, cracked, or bent anything.

At first, I thought I was imagining the tiny spirals of smoke oozing from inside the rounded symbols. When they skimmed across my skin and coiled around my wrist, I started to panic and shake my hand. When they slithered higher and circled my neck, I tried to scream. The panic tightening my chest constricted my throat, transforming my screech into a quivering squeak.

I couldn't move, could barely breathe. I was frozen in place like a statue and forced to watch the pulsing tentacles cover my entire body until I looked like a life-size bubble of warm glowing goo. This was it. I was finally having a paranormal experience and was going to die before I could tell my father he was right.

No matter how much I gulped, I couldn't get enough air into my lungs to keep my vision from blurring. With a shimmering burst of brilliant blue light and a strangled gasp, darkness descended, and me along with it.

***

"Rylee, can you hear me? Are you all right?" If I was dead, why was I hearing my grandmother's voice, and why did it sound like an amplified bull horn on the edge of hysterics? An annoying shake of my shoulder pulled me further from my hazy state. My eyelids twitched, fluttered a few times, then spread apart. Grams was on her knees hovering over me, concern and a hint of moisture lining her eyes.

"Oh, thank goodness," she exclaimed, relaxing back on her haunches. "What happened? Do you want me to take you to the hospital? Jade is still here. I can close the shop, and we can go right now. Or maybe calling you an ambulance would be better?"

"Grams." My voice sounded as if sawdust had gotten wedged inside my throat. I swallowed several times, then tried again. "I'm fine." At least I thought I was okay, until I noticed I was lying on the floor next to my desk. My brain was a little slow to catch up, but when it did, when I remembered what happened with the spirit seeker, my pulse accelerated and I jolted into an upright position. A bad move according to my blurred vision and the pain thumping against my temples. I took several deep breaths, then checked my entire body to make sure the snaky blue tendrils were really gone.

It took a few more seconds for me to realize the spirit seeker was no longer glued to my palm. "Where is it?" The last thing I wanted was for Grams to find the wooden cylinder and suffer through the same horrible experience.

"Where is what?" Grams glanced around, her gaze locking on the obelisk lying on the floor under the desk and looking totally harmless. "You mean this?" She reached for the piece of wood.

"No, don't!" I screeched, making an ineffective attempt to grab her arm with my quivering hand.

"Honestly, Rylee, what is wrong with you?" Grams tsked, clutching the seeker on one end and waving it in front of my face. "It's only a stick of wood."

Yeah, a deadly stick of wood. Or was it? I couldn't believe nothing happened when Grams touched it. Had I imagined the whole I'm-being-attacked-by-a-paranormal-element thing? Had I finally reached the point where refusing to embrace my family's acceptance of the unknown had forced me to have one whopping hallucination before losing consciousness?

I certainly hoped that wasn't the case. I didn't want to be the first member of our family to be classified as certifiably insane. Okay, I wouldn't be the first. There was a crazy ancestor somewhere on my father's side, but no one ever talked about her. Much.

"Is everything okay in here?" Jade appeared in the doorway, clutching the frame. "Rylee, what are you doing on the floor?" She gripped the doorframe. "You didn't fall out of your chair again, did you?"

"No," I groaned. Now was really not the time to be reminded about my occasional propensity for miscalculating the distance between my backside and the chair's seat.

"Let's get you off the floor, then you can tell us what happened." After Grams set the seeker on the desk, she helped me to my feet, then gently eased me into the nearest chair. "Jade, why don't you make her a cup of

Caroline's special herbal tea? There's a container in the cabinet above the sink in the break room."

"On it," Jade said, doing a spin and heading back into the hallway.

My mother had a cure for everything. Some of the townsfolk raved about her herbal remedies, even considered them legendary.

"Are you sure you don't want me to take you to the hospital?" Grams slid the chair from the corner closer to me and sat down. "I could call Dr. Green's office. I'm sure if you explained what happened, he'd get you in right away."

I gave her a weak smile. "I don't need to see a doctor." How could I tell a medical professional that I'd been attacked by a stick and a blue light, then not expect them to reserve a special room in a private facility for me. A room filled with padded walls accompanied by years of psychiatric therapy.

"I'll be fine." Though the pounding in my head indicated otherwise, I tried to sound convincing. "I just have a headache." I rubbed the back of my head and winced at the small knot on my scalp, no doubt the result of my head connecting with the floor when I fell.

A few minutes later, the click of heels announced Jade's return. "This should help." She handed me one of the spare coffee cups we kept in the employees' break room.

"Thanks." I wrinkled my nose at the steaming liquid's less than favorable shade of green. I'd had plenty of my mother's concoctions over the years, and this wasn't a color I recognized. Nor did I believe the ingredients inside the cup included the teaspoon or two of honey my mother added to enhance the flavor and make her unusual drinks easier to swallow. "Are you sure you made it correctly?" I sniffed the richly spiced lemon aroma and didn't detect anything out of the ordinary.

Jade rolled her eyes. "I know it looks bad, but I followed the instructions on the container." She pushed a stack of papers aside and perched on the edge of the desk. "And before you ask, the last customer left before I came back to check on you."

Jade was always good at knowing what I was thinking and how much I worried about the business now that my parents had made running it my responsibility. I relaxed and settled into the chair, knowing the bell would inform us if someone came into the shop.

I took a sip of the brew, which surprisingly didn't taste too bad. After several swallows, my shaky motor skills returned to normal and the throbbing in my head slowly subsided.

I glanced from Jade to Grams, who were patiently waiting for me to explain how I ended up on the floor. I didn't want my grandmother to worry, but I knew better than to keep the truth from her, abbreviated or otherwise. Even so, I'd wait until I was alone with Jade and Shawna before sharing the worst of the unpleasant details.

"I'm not entirely sure what happened." I steadied the cup on my lap and pointed at the chest sitting in the disarray on my desk. "Mom said she was sending chocolates, so I thought the bag inside the case was filled with candy." I ignored Jade's indignant snort, her way of letting me know I was a terrible friend for not offering to share.

"Let me see that." Grams held her hand out to Jade, then inspected the words inscribed on the inside of the lid. "And after reading the warning, you opened it because..." She followed with one of her condescending glares.

"I thought it was a cute marketing blurb." Not a precursor to a life-threatening event. "How was I supposed to know it was going to zap me?"

"When you say zapped, do you mean a staticky jolt or like being struck by lightning, only without dying?" Jade snickered sarcastically.

"Neither, I was attacked by the blue tendrils of death, and I'm lucky to be alive."

"This is what happens when you don't believe," Grams said.

I slumped my shoulders because any protest would be moot. Thankfully, the bell on the door tinkled, interrupting any further lectures.

"I've got it." Grams patted my shoulder on her way out of the room. "Oh, and Rylee," she called from the doorway.

"Yeah."

"I'm glad you're all right, but you should call your father and tell him what happened."

"She's right. You could have been hurt...badly," Jade said.

"I know." My parents had been looking forward to this trip for years, my mother more than my father. The last thing I wanted to do was call and upset my father. Or worse, make his day and have him rush home to investigate the spirit seeker further.

"Why don't you try standing?" Jade offered me a hand and helped me out of the chair. My knees no longer wobbled, and with the help of the desk, I was able to take a few steps without landing on the floor. Once I was upright and managing on my own, Jade pulled the cardboard box onto her lap and dug through the remaining Styrofoam.

"Ah-ha." She held up a cellophane-wrapped box with the words "Assorted Milk and Dark Chocolates" embossed in bright yellow lettering across the top. She also pulled out a sheet of paper and, after unfolding it and reading what was printed on it, handed it to me. "Maybe you should try calling this Madame Minerva person first."

***

After finishing the lukewarm burger and fries Jade brought me from the cantina, I figured Madame Minerva had some explaining to do, so I reached for my phone.

The first thing I wanted to know was how she got away with selling something as dangerous as the spirit seeker. Or at least why there wasn't a better warning label plastered all over it. Something that clearly stated that handling the product resulted in being attacked by the blue tentacles of death.

My phone chimed before I had a chance to key in the numbers. I saw my father's name on the screen and tapped the accept icon. "Hey…"

"Rylee, did you get a chance to open your birthday present yet?" He asked excitedly. "I received a notification that the package was delivered. We weren't allowed to use our phones during the haunted house tour; otherwise, I would've called you sooner."

Birthday? I shuffled my fingers through my hair, careful to avoid the tender spot on the back of my scalp. "Dad, my birthday isn't for another two months." I pinched the bridge of my nose. My father had a horrendous memory for dates. If not for my suspicious nature and the fact that many of the gifts I'd received were detrimental to my health, I'd be thrilled that my father wanted to celebrate my birthday more than once a year.

"Don't worry, sweetie." My mother's melodic voice came through the speaker. No doubt she was hovering close by so she could talk on the phone. "I'm sure your father will find another gift for you by the time your birthday arrives."

Truly, another present wasn't necessary. Not if it was anything like the spirit seeker, or any of the other magically inclined gifts I'd received in celebration of my birth. People would lose sleep if I told them about some of the things my father had given me. Not to mention the items he ordered online, saying he wanted to test their magical abilities so he could sell them to customers.

I was a practiced professional at making the items I considered dangerous disappear. One of the top shelves in the storeroom was packed with the boxes I used to hide them.

I'd spent many birthdays over the years wishing my father would have gotten me a doll or a pair of pink bunny slippers. Heck, I'd have been happy if I'd gotten a plastic dinosaur collection, anything remotely similar to what the other kids got from their parents.

I knew my father meant well, and voicing my opinion would only hurt his feelings. Protesting against receiving another present wouldn't do any good either, so I remained silent, hoping they'd forget the upcoming day that marked my arrival into the world.

"Did you see any ghosts? And, do they look like zombies?" he asked.

I heard my mother's tsk and knew she was mimicking one of Grams's eye rolls.

I assumed he was still talking about my gift and wondered why any parent would want to give their child something designed to produce nightmarish creatures. "Sorry, Dad. No ghosts. No zombies."

"Well, that's disappointing," he grumbled. "I thought for sure when I saw it, and got one of my feelings, that buying it for you was important."

I wasn't disappointed, not even a little. I wished whenever the other members of my family got their so-called feelings, they'd ignore them, at least the ones that included me and anything paranormal. I took a deep breath, then released a heavy sigh, choosing not to encourage him with details of the blue tendrils. Changing the subject always worked. "What time does the cruise leave tomorrow?"

"What? Oh." I imagined him rubbing the balding spot on the top of his head. Something he did whenever he got distracted.

"We'll be boarding around noon and leaving in the afternoon." My mother had officially taken over the call. No doubt because my father was pouting since his gift hadn't worked. At least not in the way he'd expected.

"How's everything going at the shop? Any problems?"

"No, everything is fine."

"And Grams?" she asked, an unspoken insinuation about my grandmother's troublemaking tendencies in her voice.

"No problems." At least none I wanted to share. My mother strongly supported Grams's theories on reincarnation. She'd be thrilled to hear about Howard and his ghostly quest. Personally, if he really was sent here to help, I thought he was doing a terrible job. Otherwise, His Furriness would have found a way to stop me from being zapped by the spirit seeker.

"We'll be back in a week, so if you run into any trouble, you can always ask Mattie for help," she said.

"Okay." Like that was ever going to happen. There were times when Mattie could be a bigger instigator than Grams.

"I need to go. Your father got us last-minute tickets for a haunted cemetery tour." My mother wasn't a fan of graveyards either, and her indifferent tone said she'd have more fun staying in her room and watching old black-and-white movies.

A snappy remark or a giggle would only earn me a reprimand, so I said, "Sounds fun, love you both and have a great trip," before disconnecting the call.

CHAPTER FIVE

Other than the few times I'd been frustrated after calling the number for Madame Minerva's and getting the voice mail, the rest of the afternoon had been relatively uneventful and pleasant, with a steady flow of customers.

After locking up for the day, I went to my apartment to grab a quick sandwich. Home being the upper level of the building, which my parents had converted into a rental apartment years ago. A rent-free apartment I'd inherited as a graduation present that came with two stipulations. One, I managed the shop when my parents traveled. And two, I made sure my grandmother stayed out of trouble in their absence. Lately, I'd found the first part of the provision to be way easier than the second.

While I ate, I stared at the seaside print hanging above the sofa and thought about the artist who'd captured the ocean using soft blues and greens. It was a gift from Roger Nelson, the previous tenant, who'd passed away from a heart attack.

He was a nice yet persnickety old man who'd never married and kept to himself. The only time I remembered seeing him in the shop was when he came down to complain about the noise from the bell. In all the years I'd been living here, I'd never heard the slightest tinkle. So either he had exceptional hearing or tormenting my family, mostly Grams, had been his favorite pastime.

His life had ended while he'd been eating an ice cream cone during his daily walk in the park. Not that I'd wished for his demise, but it would have been hard to accept my parents' generous offer if I'd had to imagine his corpse being found inside my home. It also saved me from having my father insist we have weekly séances in my living room so he could attempt to speak with Roger's spirit.

I drained the last few swallows of my bottled water and looked at the time on my cell. The committee meeting started at seven thirty, and it was nearing six. I had just enough time to drive across town to pick up Jade and Shawna since they'd appointed me as the official chauffeur. Grams had made arrangements to ride with Mattie and promised to meet me there later.

The drive was enjoyable, the additional traffic from visiting tourists minimal and giving me the opportunity to unwind. I loved this time of day. The fading sunlight filled the sky with brilliant pinks and yellows. I rolled my window down, inhaled the briny smell of the ocean, and let the cool breeze tease the ends of my dark hair.

It wasn't long before I was parking my car on the street near the front entrance to the tan two-story building where Jade and Shawna shared an apartment. They were outside and sitting on the concrete steps waiting for me.

They had both changed into casual pants and shirts. Jade's top was a teal a few shades lighter than her heels. Shawna's was a shade of purple to match her new hairdo. I wondered what she was going to do with all the clothes she purchased two months ago to go with her previously pink strands. On the upside, if she ever decided to use more than one color in her hair at a time, she could accessorize any way she liked.

It wasn't surprising to see Bryce, Jade's older brother, sitting with them on the bottom step. Nor was it unusual to see his tall frame hunched over the laptop computer sitting on his lap. He spent more time at their place than he did at his own. Jade and I always suspected he had a thing for Shawna, though we were pretty sure she was oblivious to how he felt.

Bryce might share similar facial features to his sister, but their personalities were very different. Jade was more outgoing while Bryce was calm and laid back. His hair color leaned more toward a light brown with golden highlights and his eyes had a brandy colored hue. When it came to clothing, he was more like me: worn jeans and old shirts. Today's pair of pants even sported a hole in one knee.

As usual, he was focused on the computer screen and only half listening to Jade and Shawna's conversation. Judging by the deepening frown on Jade's face, I'd say whatever they were discussing was on its way to becoming an argument. Not an uncommon event since they had opposing views on anything from favorite rock bands to the best conditioner to use on their hair.

They also had no problem sharing their viewpoints and handing out advice on a whim. Advice mostly aimed in my direction, which usually included enhancing my wardrobe, changing my hair color, and the best tips for dating a guy. None of which I willingly solicited.

When you had friends who were closer than sisters, it meant every aspect of your life—secrets included—was open for scrutiny. Thankfully, the secrets went no further than the three of us, a pact that included never revealing anything we shared with members of our family.

If my parents hadn't wanted someone they could trust living in the apartment above the shop, I'd have ended up sharing living quarters with my friends. At the moment, having a place to myself held a lot of appeal.

If I didn't want to be late for the meeting, I needed to play referee. With a heavy sigh, I got out of the car and headed up the short sidewalk lined with pink and white azaleas. "Hey, guys." I raised my voice when I realized they hadn't noticed me.

Shawna jerked her head in my direction. "Are you okay?" She hopped to her feet and dashed across the few feet of concrete separating us to pull me into a hug. Apparently, whatever topic they'd been discussing wasn't nearly as important as my arrival.

Shawna released the tight grip on my neck. "Jade told me about what happened at the shop. About the…" She turned to Jade. "What was it you called the thing that zapped her?"

"A spirit seeker," I muttered, then glanced at Bryce. Outside of his teacher's assistant job at the Cumberpatch Cove Community College, he was the proud leader of the Supernatural Spoof Squashers. It was a small group of geeky individuals, one he'd organized, whose sole purpose was to investigate anything otherworldly in Cumberpatch and a few of the neighboring towns. I wouldn't be surprised if my father was an honorary member.

"What's a spirit seeker?" Bryce jerked his attention away from the screen, his eyes sparkling with curiosity.

I inwardly groaned. I wasn't in the mood to be interrogated, nor did I want Bryce and his group showing up at the shop ready to investigate what had happened to me. "Nothing important. Just some old thing my dad sent me." I shot Jade a pleading look, knowing she'd understand without me having to say anything.

Shawna, on the other hand, needed a more direct approach. I slipped my arm through hers and tugged her in the direction of my car. "We need to get going. You know how Serena gets if anyone is late."

"Are you sure you should be going to the meeting?" Shawna asked, dragging her feet.

I relished any excuse not to attend and was tempted to say no. I didn't mind helping out with community events. It was having to deal with the Abbott sisters and their tendency to suck the enjoyment out of volunteering, or anything else they were involved with. If I knew for certain my mother wouldn't hear about my absence or that Lavender wouldn't make something up and broadcast it to her buddies on the gossip circuit, I'd head home right now. "I'm fine. My headache is gone." The lump on the back of my head was smaller but still there, information I decided to keep to myself.

"Well, if you're sure." Shawna crinkled her nose, not totally convinced.

"She's sure." Jade came to my rescue and nudged Shawna to pick up her pace.

"Wait, I have more questions." Bryce closed his laptop and set it on the step next to him.

"Sorry, bro, they'll have to wait. See you later." Jade called over her shoulder.

Scrunching his face with his arms crossed over his chest wasn't a good look for Bryce. It made me worry he wasn't going to give up on finding out more about the spirit seeker.

The calm I'd gained from my pleasurable drive was gone. I spent part of the trip listening to Jade and Shawna discuss plans for the weekend and the remainder convincing myself that the next two hours weren't going to be as bad as the tightly twisted knot in my stomach suggested. In order to stay positive, I reminded myself that the Founders Day celebration scheduled for Saturday was only four days away. It meant that this was the last committee meeting I'd have to attend for another year.

***

I turned onto Treasure Lane a half hour before the meeting was due to start and followed the winding road to the Beaumont Inn. The three-story Victorian home resembling a Southern mansion was located on a bluff overlooking a breathtaking stretch of coastline near the outskirts of town. It had been transformed by one of the

Beaumonts' ancestors into a beautiful bed-and-breakfast type establishment. It had a plush, dark green lawn, complete with well-maintained flower beds and trimmed hedges that ran along the front of the building.

Colin Beaumont, the current owner, came from one of the few families in the area who never had to worry about money. During high school, there'd been no better catch than him. He was an athlete, and though he'd been popular with all the girls, Serena Abbott had been the lucky one to snare him. Having a husband who was a wealthy man came with perks and made her one of the inn's owners. It also meant, as head of the Founders Day committee, she got to choose where the meetings were held.

I didn't mind the location as much as I did having to deal with Lavender. Going to the inn was like being on a sports team, traveling out of state and knowing you wouldn't have the home team advantage.

The inn itself was a beautiful building with a lot of history. It had nice meeting rooms with comfortable cushioned chairs, not the folding metal ones where your backside went to sleep after twenty minutes of sitting on the hard surface.

The best part of the whole evening was the assortment of goodies Serena had Mattie's shop cater for every meeting. Since I'd missed out on my muffin earlier today, my mouth watered in anticipation of the two fancy pastries I planned to eat. I followed Jade and Shawna into the lobby, saw Lavender standing behind the reservation desk chatting with Molly Jacobs, Al's baby sister, and decided I might need three of anything covered in chocolate to make it through the night.

We'd almost escaped attention when Shawna stopped to wave at Molly. The young girl grinned and waved back. Lavender faked a smile for the benefit of the couple who'd entered right behind us.

Shawna looped her arm through mine. "I can't believe

this is our last meeting already, can you?"

"Sure can't," I muttered, certain that getting a root canal would be more fun than tonight's meeting. After three years of working the annual event, I still didn't understand Shawna's enthusiasm. I knew from experience she'd be ten times worse during the annual pirate festival in the fall.

"Oh, come on." Jade draped her arm across my shoulder. "You know you can't wait for the treasure hunt. Admit it."

"No." *Well, maybe.* Okay, there was a part of me that enjoyed solving puzzles. I refused to admit that unraveling the clues on the treasure map handed out to all participants had been a lot of fun.

"Uh-huh," Jade said.

"I think it's going to be great," Shawna said. "The chests you got are way better than the ones we had last year."

"Thanks." I had to admit I was pretty proud of them. I thought about the chest Jessica had given me and smiled. It didn't matter if I finished the hunt or not. I already had one of the treasures.

We reached the end of the hallway and found the double doors leading into the meeting room already open. The room was trimmed with white molding, and large wood-framed pictures of seascapes hung in the middle of three pastel-yellow walls. Long rectangular tables seating six chairs each were set up in five rows in a classroom-style arrangement. Serena was at the front of the room standing next to a speaker's podium, arranging a stack of papers. She gave us a brief nod before returning her attention to what she was doing.

Some of the chairs were already occupied by other committee members. Edith and Joyce Haverston, the owners of the Classic Broom, were sitting in a row near the front. The sisters were in their forties and had never married. One was blonde, the other brunette, and both kept their long hair loose and at a length that reached the small of their backs. Whether they wore dresses or pants, black was the prominent color of their wardrobe.

My father was convinced they were practicing witches, and there were times when my friends and I agreed with him.

It had been a while since I'd been in their shop. Shortly after a breakup, Shawna was convinced that turning her ex-boyfriend into a lower life-form would make her feel better and had talked Jade and me into visiting the store and checking out their wide selection of potions. At the time, it had worried me how convincing Edith sounded when she informed us that transformation spells didn't come in a pill or liquid form.

Luckily, I'd been able to coax Shawna out of the shop after she'd purchased some scented candles and a carton of chocolates guaranteed to cure a broken heart. I love sweets, but that was one box of yummies I'd refused to sample.

Sitting a couple of rows behind the sisters was Robert Wilson, also known as Bob, the owner of Barnacle Bob's Books. His shiny bald head reflected the overhead lights. His shoulders were hunched, his focus on the screen of his phone, his thumbs moving rapidly as he composed a text. He took a break from typing to push his dark-rimmed plastic glasses up the bridge of his nose, then shook his head at whatever response he'd received.

On the other end of the room were two long buffet tables draped with a dark blue tablecloth that matched one of the colors in the patterned tan carpet. Brant Delaney, owner of the cantina where Shawna worked, had also arrived and was pouring himself a cup of coffee from one of the four insulated carafes sitting between rows of clean cups and glasses.

"Ladies," he said, tipping his head in our direction and giving us one of his charming smiles. In his early thirties, with short cropped blond hair and blue eyes, the man was in amazing shape and was responsible for breaking a few hearts in our community. His extracurriculars aside, his restaurant was by far one of the best places to eat in Cumberpatch.

"Hey, Brant," I said, squelching the urge to flirt, only because I knew better and didn't want a lecture from Shawna about it later. I followed my friends to an empty row of chairs in the middle of the section. We'd learned the hard way to get our seats right away, then worry about grabbing a snack. The back three rows of tables filled up first. Anyone who sat in the first two rows was fair game when Serena couldn't get volunteers and decided to do some self-appointing.

After shedding our jackets and draping them over the backs of our chairs, we headed toward the beverage table where Brant was standing, sipping his coffee. I glanced past him at the goodies table and was disappointed to see several stacks of plates, plenty of napkins and utensils, but no baked delectables. It was then that I realized I hadn't seen Grams or Mattie yet. It wasn't like them to be late. I was just about to pull the cell out of my purse and call when they walked into the room, slightly winded, their arms loaded with large sealed plastic containers.

"Sorry we're late," Mattie nervously said to Serena, then headed for the table.

"It's all right." Serena followed up her comment with an exasperated sigh, then glanced at the thin-banded gold watch on her wrist. "Ten minutes, everyone, so if you want something to eat, please get it now."

Brant set his cup next to a carafe. "Here, let me help you with that." He took the three containers Mattie was holding and placed them on the adjoining table.

"Thanks," she said, pulling the strap of the purse dangling near her elbow back up on her shoulder.

Grams set the two containers she was carrying on the table, then gave my arm a worried squeeze. "Everything okay?"

My grandmother and I might not agree on some things, but the additional concern in her voice was reassuring. Asking the generalized question was her way of checking to make sure I was still doing okay after my near-death or whatever the heck kind of experience I'd had earlier without mentioning the spirit seeker in public.

"Super, or at least it will be after I, oooh"—I stepped around Grams to drool over the plate Mattie had just uncovered—"have one of those double fudge brownies."

"Did she say brownies?" Jade's head snapped in my direction, her drink forgotten as she rushed to be next in line.

"Mattie, these cookies look great." Shawna snatched two of them off the platter, not bothering to use a plate.

Jade frowned, shook her head, and handed Shawna a napkin.

"What?" Shawna placed one of the cookies on the white cloth, then took a bite out of the other.

"Good evening, everyone." Serena's voice rang through the overhead speaker system. "Why don't we get started."

The few people who'd been standing around visiting ended their conversations and shuffled toward their seats. Lavender picked that moment to waltz through the entryway and stroll toward the podium. She took a seat in the front row closest to her sister, then shifted in her chair and expectantly glared in my direction. I glared back, then returned to what I was doing—filling my plate.

There were plenty of goodies on the trays, so I didn't feel guilty about the two extra brownies I snatched before filling a cup with coffee and following Jade back to our table. Shawna had already taken her seat and was leaning on the table, talking to Edith, who was sitting in the row in front of her. Jade slid in next to Shawna. I took the chair on her right, and Brant sat at the table behind us.

"Thank you all for coming." Serena scanned the crowd before continuing. "I'm sure you all heard about Lyle Crumpet's tragic death."

A low rumble of murmurs filled the room with people sharing their thoughts. The remarks ranged from disbelief to those who were convinced the accusations about Lyle were true. Serena silenced the crowd by tapping her microphone, the shrill static filling the air. "You'll all be glad to know that Bob has agreed to take over Lyle's duties."

Bob looked up from his phone long enough to acknowledge her praise and pretend he was paying attention.

Serena continued the meeting, the next twenty minutes spent on a recap of Saturday's itinerary. I already knew there'd be a midmorning parade, vendor booths, and a small carnival for kids set up on the plaza. Thanks to my mother volunteering me to help with the treasure hunt, I'd barely escaped being stuck serving food for most of the day. After listening to Serena's long list of what those working the booths could and couldn't do, I decided to give my mother a huge thank-you when she got back from her cruise.

By the time I'd consumed two more brownies and another cup of coffee, I had plenty of sugar and caffeine running through my veins. Besides being antsy and unable to sit for very long without twitching, I couldn't stop thinking about Lyle and his mysterious death. I still didn't believe he was guilty and silently pondered the possibilities of what had happened.

If there was anyone in town who'd have more information about Lyle, it would be Brant. Being a restaurant owner with the ability to charm the locals, he was tapped into the heartbeat of the gossiping community. I was about to turn and ask him if he'd heard anything when Serena asked Jessica to give her status report.

When Jessica didn't respond, I glanced around the room and didn't see her familiar face anywhere in the crowd. Now that I thought about it, I hadn't seen her when we arrived either.

"Maybe she's still at the cemetery, or maybe she got lost," Lavender responded with her usual sarcasm.

Jessica, lost in the cemetery? I didn't think so. She was the best tour guide they'd had in years. I'd bet if there was a contest to recite the name on every tombstone, she'd win.

"Or maybe it took her longer than expected to finish hiding the chests." After receiving death glares from both the Abbott sisters, I realized coming to Jessica's defense hadn't scored me any points.

"This is unacceptable." Serena's face flushed dark crimson, and she gripped the edges of the podium. "She should have called if she was going to be late. This is our last meeting, and we needed that information."

A tingle of dread zipped along my spine. It wasn't like Jessica to miss a meeting. She would at least call if she was going to be late.

Jade leaned toward me and whispered, "What do you think happened to her?"

"I don't know." And I hoped nothing after remembering Jessica's upsetting conversation with the guy in the hoodie. Just in case, I pulled out my phone and sent her a quick text. A couple of minutes passed without a response, so I sent another message. Still nothing.

I thought about slipping into the hall to call Jessica directly, but had drawn enough attention to myself for one night.

Serena referred to her notes. "Greg, can you tell us where you're at with setting up the display we had designed for the museum?"

Since most of the tourists who came for the celebration usually visited his museum, he'd volunteered to set up a large cardboard display in his lobby. When Greg didn't answer, Serena perused the crowd with a frustrating glare. "He's not here either. Well, this is…" She huffed.

"I'm here." Greg eased into the room through the main door leading into the hallway. His normally impeccably styled hair was mussed and his cotton shirt was wrinkled. "Sorry I'm late, I had problems with my car." He let the door close behind him, then took a seat in the front row near Lavender. Not that he had a choice; the rest of the chairs were already taken.

Serena rolled her eyes, dismissing Greg's personal problems as unimportant. "We need an update on the display."

"Yes…sure." Greg swiped his hand through his hair, smoothing the loose strands back into place. "It arrived yesterday, and I set it up this morning. So far, we've gotten a lot of great feedback from the people who've seen it. Many of them said they'd be staying through the weekend and planned to attend Saturday's events."

"That is good news." The rigid line of Serena's shoulders softened. "Thank you."

From that point, the discussions turned to recaps of everything I'd heard before. I spent the remainder of my time only half listening to the meeting, too busy wondering what had happened to Jessica.

CHAPTER SIX

It was nearing nine thirty by the time the meeting ended and I'd dropped Shawna and Jade back at their apartment. I hadn't received a return text from Jessica, and the call I'd made from the inn had gone straight to voice mail.

The antsy feeling I'd developed during the meeting was growing steadily stronger. She wasn't a close friend, and other than the things she'd shared with me when visiting the shop, I didn't know her very well. Even so, it didn't stop me from worrying about her or realizing I wasn't going to get any sleep until I knew she was all right.

I didn't know where she lived, but before I tracked down an address, I decided to drive by the cemetery and see if her car was parked in the visitor lot. If it was, then I'd worry about getting inside to find her since it was long past visiting hours and the main gates were probably locked.

I wanted to believe the reason she wasn't answering was simple, so during the drive, I mentally reviewed all the plausible things that might have caused her to miss the meeting. I ruled out the possibility of Jessica getting hurt. The cemetery might be a large, sometimes spooky place, but for the most part, it was safe. She'd worked there long enough to know every tombstone, crypt, and inch of real estate in the place.

Maybe it took her longer to hide the chests than she'd thought, or maybe she was having car problems, or maybe my annoying tingle was right and she was in serious trouble. I groaned, irritated that all the reasons I'd come up with so far weren't viable enough to prevent Jessica from answering my texts or returning my call.

I was back to wondering if the guy I'd seen her with earlier in the day had turned out to be a stalker. What if he'd followed her to the cemetery to continue their discussion? What if things got out of hand and Jessica really had gotten hurt?

My stomach tightened into a queasy knot. I'd been so focused on the what-ifs that I hadn't noticed the street light change to red and had to slam on the brakes to stop from cruising through a busy intersection.

Once the light turned green, I turned left toward the cemetery. There weren't many homes or businesses along the street, so traffic was light, and eventually, my vehicle ended up being the only one on the road. Streetlights were sparse, and the trees lining the undeveloped properties on either side of the two lane road were cast in heavy shadows.

Other than the lights on the dashboard, everything inside my car was dark. Dark except for the soft glow that suddenly materialized in the passenger seat. The transparent bubble of light grew brighter and began to form a shape. Within seconds, the shape transformed into Jessica, or a version of Jessica with a luminescent glow in the same brilliant blue as the snaky things I'd seen coming out of the spirit seeker. She was wearing the same outfit, a nice button-down blouse, skirt, and half-inch black flats she'd been wearing this morning, although the unadorned baseball cap was new and the same blue as the rest of her.

Dividing my attention between the road and the

passenger seat, I tightened my grip on the steering wheel and blinked. Jessica didn't disappear. Instead, she turned her head and pinned me with pleading eyes. "Rylee, I need your help." Her grief-stricken voice filled the air.

Besides the jolt to my heart and the ringing in my ears I'd caused by shrieking, several things happened at once.

Jessica shouted, "Look out!"

A truck pulled in front of me from a side street. I swerved to the right to miss him, then hit the brakes and skidded to a stop in the gravel. My maneuvering abilities weren't great, but at least I hadn't damaged my car or been injured. The other driver wasn't as lucky. He'd missed a lamppost, but the front end of his vehicle ended up in the ditch across the street. All I could see were the bright red brake lights and the reflection they made on the dark tailgate.

"Rylee, what if the other driver is hurt? Maybe you should help him."

Me not screaming because a spirit was talking to me as if it was something we did every day was unexpected. I assumed it was because I'd spent my life with a father, friends, and a town whose inhabitants were convinced the supernatural existed. Otherwise, I was certain I'd have handled the situation with a greater amount of hysteria.

As it was, I squeaked and scooted closer to my door, jamming my eyelids shut, hoping I was having a massive hallucination. It took what seemed like hours, but was only a few seconds for me to gulp in enough air to remain conscious. Although, if I passed out, maybe she'd be gone when I woke up.

"Rylee, I'm serious. You should go," Jessica scolded.

I slowly opened one eye, then the other. Jessica, who wasn't the flesh-and-blood person I'd spoken with this morning, was calmly sitting in my passenger seat, but now she had her arms crossed and was staring at me expectantly. My brain finally engaged, reconciling the fact that she had died and she was definitely a ghost. A deep sorrow rippled through me, and I blinked again to keep the threatening tears from trickling down my face.

"Jessica, are you… What happened?" I curled my fingers, squelching the urge to reach across the seat and swipe my hand through her body. Why did people, me especially, always want to touch things when they didn't know what they were? If I ended up with some kind of slimy goo dripping from my hand, I was either going to freak out or lose all the sweets I'd eaten earlier.

"Later. Right now, you need to help the person in the truck." She emphasized her remark by sternly pointing across the street.

Sometimes, in the face of the unknown, I can be a little slow to react. Not to mention a little embarrassed that I needed a ghost to be my voice of reason. I wasn't sure what the proper protocol was for dealing with a spirit's demands, but she was obviously right, and finding out what happened to her would have to wait. "Yeah…okay." With shaky hands, I unfastened my seat belt.

"Stay here." Pretending I was in control never hurt when I was wavering on the line between reality and questioning my own sanity. Besides, I didn't know how the person in the truck would react if Jessica decided to float, walk, or do whatever ghosts did and followed me.

My knees were a little wobbly, and getting out of the car wasn't exactly a graceful effort. Once I could stand without using the car for support, I checked the street to make sure I wasn't going to end up as an ornament adorning someone else's hood.

I'd barely taken two steps when a man appeared near the edge of the embankment. He didn't seem to be injured, but it never hurt to check. "Are you all right?" I hurried the remainder of the way across the street.

He met my gaze with piercing brown eyes the color of whiskey. "That depends." He stepped onto the shoulder, straightening to his full height, which towered over mine by at least eight inches. His tan suede jacket showed some wear, and the faded jeans and boots were a natural fit and a good look on him.

I had to admit he was handsome in a brooding, intense, suspicious kind of way. I ignored my quickened pulse and focused on my curiosity. "On what?"

"On whether or not you have a habit of running other drivers off the road."

"Not usually." I bit my lower lip, trying not to overreact to his insinuation. Technically, I might have been driving near the middle of the road, but if he hadn't pulled out in front of me, he wouldn't have needed to swerve to miss me. Since I wasn't the only one involved in our near-miss incident, I wasn't about to take all the blame or stay silent on the subject. "Where were you going in such a hurry that you didn't bother to stop?" I pointed at the stop sign he'd purposely neglected to heed.

"I was headed to a crime scene."

"A crime scene, seriously?" I scoffed, calling his bluff. I knew most of our local law enforcement, had grown up with some of them, and didn't recall ever meeting this guy.

"Seriously." He reached into the back pocket of his jeans and pulled out a leather wallet, then flipped it open to show me a badge.

Even with the overhead light, I still had to squint to see the information. The word BANGOR in all caps was etched into the glossy gold at the bottom of the shield and was the only important detail I got before he quickly snapped the leather shut, then returned it to his pocket.

Bangor was at least an hour and a half drive away. Unless he was on vacation, which would explain why he was driving the nice truck and not a car, but it didn't explain why he was on his way to check out a murder.

We had our share of crime, but nothing that our local sheriff or one of his deputies couldn't handle. At least I didn't think so. "You're quite a ways from Bangor. Did you get lost, Detective?" Since he'd mentioned a crime scene and wasn't wearing a uniform, it was logical to assume he held a higher rank.

"Prescott, Detective Logan Prescott. And no, I'm not lost." He pressed his lips into a thin line, his clamped jaw causing his muscles to twitch.

It was obvious he didn't appreciate my sense of humor, so asking him why he was here investigating a crime didn't seem like a good idea.

"And you are?" He used the same you-will-tell-me-what-I-want-to-know-or-else tone my mother used on me when I was younger.

Being stubborn ran in my family, so my initial reaction was to refuse his request. Even if I didn't answer, he was in law enforcement, and Cumberpatch wasn't an oversized metropolis. He could easily find out anything he wanted to know about me, everything from where I got my hair done to the unusual antics of my family. The latter wouldn't help my current situation, not if I included the fact that I could see a ghost.

"It's Rylee Spencer."

"Well, Ms. Spencer, you were driving all over the road. How do I know you weren't involved in something you shouldn't be??" He took an intimidating step forward.

I crossed my arms, refusing to move. "Honestly, do I look like a criminal to you?"

He quirked a brow with the hint of a grin.

Maybe I'd been wrong about the brooding detective not having a sense of humor. Even so, I decided not to push it. "Never mind, don't answer that." Now would probably be a good time to change the subject. "I'm sorry about your truck. Is there any damage?" Feeling a modicum of guilt, I focused on his vehicle. I didn't see any scrapes or dings.

"No damage. It looks like you had some rain recently because the front tires are stuck in the mud."

"That's great news. Not that you're stuck but that your truck is okay." I corrected with the wave of my hand.

I slipped my cell out of my jacket pocket. "I know a

great mechanic who could be here within an hour to pull you out." *A half hour tops if I put some extra effort into begging.*

"I have a better idea. You can drive me where I need to go., and we can worry about taking care of my truck afterward." He placed his hand on my elbow and guided me across the street, then walked around to the passenger side of my car.

I thought about Jessica's ghost waiting inside the vehicle and how he would react once he saw her. "I don't know if that's such a great idea." I nervously glanced inside, relieved to see the empty seats. A relief that was quickly replaced by the concern that I'd imagined her and might be losing my mind.

Logan tapped the roof and grinned. "Is that because you're afraid I'm a serial killer and going to make off with you?"

"Nooo." Feeling more than a little embarrassed, I opened the door, released all the locks, and climbed inside. "Where exactly am I taking you?" I asked once our seat belts were secured and the engine was running.

"There's a cemetery a couple of blocks from here," he said.

Not the destination I'd expected. "I thought you said you were headed to a crime scene." I didn't think he'd be amused if I pointed out that people who were already dead and buried didn't qualify.

"Actually, it's a murder scene. And because of our incident, I'm late."

Murder. The knot in my stomach tightened even more. Logically, I was still struggling with whether or not I'd seen Jessica, but I'd read a lot of mystery novels and was good at putting clues together. I didn't need a fancy degree to know who had been murdered.

I gripped the steering wheel and blurted, "Jessica's dead," before I could stop myself.

Logan shifted in his seat, his gaze accusatory. "How did

you know the victim's name was Jessica?"

CHAPTER SEVEN

My temporary tenure as Logan's chauffeur was silent, short, and tense. If I had to guess by the studious way his gaze went from staring out the window to warily glancing at me, he was in detective mode and hadn't believed me when I told him why I'd been heading to the cemetery before our near miss on the road.

It was probably a good thing he'd chosen to intimidate me with silence, because I didn't want to answer any more of his questions, nor could I tell him how I knew who they'd found at the crime scene.

Jessica hadn't reappeared inside my vehicle or anywhere else along the way, leaving my thoughts filled with the hope my assumption was wrong. A hope that was obliterated as soon as we reached the cemetery and I got a glimpse of her car through the gaps in the black wrought-iron fencing bordering three sides of the parking lot.

Once we reached the small driveway leading into the lot, Logan said, "Pull inside and park off to the right."

The gate was open, so I did as he instructed, making sure I avoided getting anywhere near the two parked police cars with their blue lights flashing.

"Now what?" I asked.

Logan unsnapped his belt. "You come with me." He was out of the vehicle before I could tell him I was okay waiting here.

Cumberpatch had its share of teenage pranksters, treasure-seeking enthusiasts, and those who couldn't wait to find a way into the cemetery after closing hours. I was in a category all by myself, the one who thought it best to stay as far away as possible from the resting place of the dead. Even so, I got out and followed Logan.

With each reluctant step, I told myself that confirming my suspicions about Jessica was the only reason I complied, not my growing interest in the handsome detective.

Logan stopped near an area cordoned off with yellow police tape stretched between some trees. "I need you to stay right here until I come back." He gestured toward the ground to emphasize his order.

Were all city cops so bossy? "And if I don't?"

He narrowed his gaze. "I'll have one of the officers arrest you and take you down to the station."

Arrest me for what? I hadn't done anything wrong. I pursed my lips and frowned, tamping down the childish notion to take a step to the left to see if he'd follow through with his threat.

"Are you saying you think I'm a suspect?" I asked.

"You knew the victim's name without me mentioning it, and you were driving in the vicinity of the murder. So yes, Ms. Spencer, until I'm convinced otherwise, you are a suspect and I'm not letting you out of my sight."

His reasons were circumstantial at best, but there was no way to prove how I knew the dead person was Jessica. "Fine." My snort was indignant and so was the glare I leveled at him.

Logan turned, but not before I caught a glimpse of his amused grin. "I'm here to see Sheriff Dixon." He showed his badge to a young officer whose name I didn't know, but who'd been posted to keep stray observers from getting too close. Logan ducked underneath the tape and walked along a path between some headstones to join the other law enforcement officials gathered around the crime scene. Out of the small group, I recognized Roy, the sheriff, and Elliott Barnes, one of his deputies.

"Rylee." Jessica appeared next to me, and I jumped. It took all my self-control not to scream for the second time tonight. Since the officer gave me a brief smile, then went back to scanning the perimeter and handling some new arrivals, I was certain I was the only one who could see her.

She sounded upset and confused. I wanted to console her and reacted without thinking by reaching for her arm. My hand passed through air, an ice-cold chill rippling across my skin. What little warmth my jacket provided was gone in an instant. After immediately pulling away, then rubbing my arms to stop from shivering, I mentally checked the "yes" box that spirits were walking freezer units. There was no way I was going to do that again, not if I could help it.

"Jessica, are you…" Asking her if she was okay probably wasn't the best idea I'd ever had. "What I mean is…"

"I'm really dead, aren't I?" It didn't look like she could form real tears, but it didn't stop her from sobbing and making loud hiccupping noises.

"I'm so sorry, but yes." Though I was relieved she'd brought the subject up first, it hadn't made confirming it any easier. For a brief moment, I wondered if being able to see Jessica was my punishment for not believing the muffin-stealing mouse was the reincarnation of my great-great uncle Howard. Or if it was a result of all the years I'd skeptically, if not quietly, scoffed at my family's beliefs. Both reasons had merit, but since I'd gone through my entire life without getting a glimpse of a ghost, I strongly believed my new ability was the result of being zapped by the spirit seeker.

After all the times my father had used me as a test subject, he'd be thrilled to know his birthday gift had worked, that he'd finally proven his theory about the existence of magic. At least when it pertained to spirits. Too bad I had no intention of sharing the information with him or anyone else until I knew what I was dealing with.

I glanced around to make sure no one was giving me a get-a-load-of-the-crazy-lady-talking-to-herself look. The officer standing sentinel was too busy fending off newly arriving bystanders to pay any attention to me. I felt a little sorry for the guy. The police might be able to keep the curious locals from entering the lot, but they wouldn't be able to keep them from parking on the street or swarming the graveyard on foot. Word traveled fast, and I wouldn't be surprised if a bunch of the visiting tourists also made an appearance.

Because of Logan, I already knew Jessica's death wasn't an accident, which meant there was a murderer running around Cumberpatch. The guy I'd seen her with earlier was the only person on my list, but I wouldn't know for sure if it was him until I asked her. Something I couldn't do without being overheard.

"Come on. Let's go over there," I whispered, then started walking, turning my head slightly to make sure she was following me. I crept along a path between some trees, stopping when I reached another long strip of police tape. From here, I got a different view of the crime scene.

Given the fact that I could see Jessica and we were standing close to more headstones, I was afraid I might be swarmed by more ghosts. "There aren't more spirits hanging around out here anywhere, are there?" The tension strumming through my body could register on the Richter scale.

"Why are you asking me? It's not like I've ever been dead before, and I'm sure I'd remember if I received a handbook or was assigned a spirit guide." Her accusatory gaze turned hopeful. "You're not a guide, are you?"

"Sorry, you're my first ghost... Ever." I didn't mention that I wanted her to be my last, or that I wished I'd wake up soon and discover all the sweets I'd eaten at the meeting had produced this nightmare.

So far, Logan had been busy studying the scene and talking to other officers. I wanted to get answers from Jessica before the situation changed and he noticed that I'd moved. "I hate to ask, but can you remember what happened or who might have wanted to do this to you?" I also wanted to ask her what the deal was with the baseball cap, since the color had changed from blue to yellow.

Jessica scrunched her nose, contemplated my question for a few seconds, then shrugged. "Other than hiding the chests for the treasure hunt, not a thing. I have no idea who would want me dead. I'm not even sure how I ended up in your car. How is it that you can see me and talk to me, but no one else can?"

I had a theory, but I wasn't in the mood to discuss my early birthday present or the irritation I was harboring for my father. "I'm not sure, but we can worry about it later. Right now we need to figure out what happened to you." Logan picked that moment to end his conversation with Sheriff Dixon. It didn't take long for his brow to furrow and his irritated gaze to move from where he'd left me to where I was standing now. Okay, so I'd moved more than a little. The least he could do was give me points for not leaving.

"Hey, Rylee, how's it going?" Startled, I squeaked and clutched my shirt. I'd been so busy having a staring contest with Logan that I hadn't noticed Troy Duncan creep around a headstone to stand next to me. His father, Keith, owned the *Swashbuckler Gazette*, the local newspaper, and Troy was their only reporter. He was a nice enough guy but could turn into a pushy bloodhound if he thought he was onto a story.

"Darn it, Troy. Don't sneak up on me like that."

"Sorry, but this is headline news." He reached into his pocket for his cell phone, then did a quick scroll across the screen with his thumb, no doubt searching for a recording app. "My sources tell me the victim was Jessica Jenkins."

"What sources?"

"I can't share that information with you." The discerning glance he gave the young officer guarding the tape was all the answer I needed. "Did you know the victim? Any idea what happened to her?"

Why does everyone assume I know something?

"Yeah, I was murdered," Jessica shrilled, the color of her cap changing to red.

I resisted the urge to turn my head, shush her, and ask her what the deal was with her hat. The last thing I needed was for Troy to see me talking to empty air. I preferred not to give the townspeople a reason to think I was crazy. Not that Lavender and some of her friends ever needed a reason when it came to my family and me.

"Are you kidding?" Not wanting to be the *Gazette*'s next headline, I pushed the phone away from my face. "Of course, I knew her. There are a lot of people in town who *knew* Jessica." I inhaled a calming breath. "I have no idea what happened to her. Why don't you go and pester Roy or Elliott? I'm sure one of them knows way more than I do."

"Already tried." He slouched, tapped the app, and shoved the phone along with his hands in his pockets. "They're not talking either." He toed the gravel walkway, a boyish attempt to win me over.

I wasn't buying it.

A murder in Cumberpatch might be the biggest story since the time someone said they saw a pirate galleon anchored in the bay, but it didn't mean I wanted to pick up the newspaper tomorrow and see my name in an embellished quote beneath a picture of Jessica's dead body.

"Rylee, everything okay over here?" I was surprised to see Greg, but thankful for the interruption.

"Greg, you knew Jessica, right?" Troy beamed, pulling out his phone again.

"No comment, Troy." Greg held up his hand. "Does your dad know you're out here harassing the locals?"

"Hey, I'm not harassing anyone. Besides, my dad says the only way to get a good story is to ask the questions no one else is willing to ask."

Greg sidestepped him to stand next to me. "I think you need to go find someone else to answer your questions."

"Geez," Troy muttered, then stomped back toward the small crowd of onlookers gathering in the area where Logan had told me to wait for him.

"Thanks, Greg," I said.

"No problem, but what are you doing out here by yourself? Where's Shawna and Jade?"

"I dropped them off already. I knew Jessica was working today, and I got worried when she didn't return my calls. I thought I'd drive by to see if she was still here."

"That was really sweet of you," Jessica said.

I tried not to smile. "That's when I saw the lights, and…" I left out the part about seeing her ghost and running Logan into a ditch. In retrospect, no one could say I didn't have a productive couple of hours.

"Decided to investigate?"

"Yeah, and you?" Other than working with each other on the committee, I didn't think Greg and Jessica were socializing friends, so what was he really doing out here?

"I…"

He didn't get a chance to finish because a man sauntered up next to him. It appeared my out-of-the-way spot wasn't as secluded as I thought. With his pirate-embossed T-shirt and sneakers, I had him pegged as a tourist long before he started to speak.

"Wow, I was planning to take one of the cemetery tours while I was here. You know, maybe see a real ghost." The tourist guy flashed a wide-toothed grin. "The guy working at the hotel registration desk didn't say anything about evening tours. Is this one of those mystery whodunit things, and if so, where do I sign up?"

I stopped myself from telling him we didn't have any *real* ghosts. I wouldn't ever be able to utter those words again. "This isn't one of those mystery things. It's an actual crime scene."

"Whoa, really?" He sounded amazed. "I thought this was going to be an average vacation. But this"—he pointed at the place where Jessica had been found—"this is exciting. Do you know who got killed?"

"Me, you jerk. What is wrong with people?" Jessica clenched her fists.

Any other time, I might have let her hit him, but I was afraid if he received a ghost's version of an icy punch, it would encourage him to stay. "She was my friend." I took a step forward, putting myself between Jessica and the tourist. When I glanced in her direction again, she was gone.

"Oh, sorry. I didn't know." The overzealous tourist caught Greg's glare. "Maybe I'll just…" He hitched his thumb toward the crowd and left.

I waited until Mr. Insensitive was out of earshot, then turned to Greg. He'd been Lyle Crumpet's employer for the last two years, ever since he'd purchased the museum. From what I could tell, they had a good working relationship. Now that we might have a few moments of uninterrupted conversation, I tried to think of the best way to ask him some questions about Lyle without sounding too nosy. It seemed strange that two people from our town had been murdered in the same week. Maybe it was a coincidence, because I couldn't think of any reason Lyle's and Jessica's deaths would be connected.

"I was sorry to hear about Lyle."

Greg's attention was drawn to something behind me. I turned and found Sheriff Roy Dixon standing on the other side of the tape, his expression grim. The silver in his dark hair was more prominent than the last time I'd seen him, and the shirt of his light tan uniform was pulled a little tighter across his midsection.

"Rylee, can I talk to you for a minute?" He lifted the tape and motioned for me to go underneath.

How was I supposed to get any answers if people kept interrupting me? Roy was a good friend of the family. Grams had gone to high school with him, and I'd known him since I was a kid. I also knew telling him no was not an option, not if I didn't want him to call my grandmother.

"Sure." To Greg, I said, "I'll see you this weekend," then ducked under the strip of plastic to follow Roy.

He led me to an area not far from the crime scene. I didn't want to see Jessica's body, yet couldn't stop staring when we passed the spot where she'd been killed. Her sheet-draped body was being wheeled away on a gurney, and some of the people who'd been swarming the site earlier were departing.

Once we were away from the other officers, Roy pressed a hand to his hip and ran his fingers through the short strands along the side of his head. I'd seen his pursed lips and disappointing frown before. Usually when Jade, Shawna, and I got caught doing something we weren't supposed to. Of course, it had been when we were younger.

I had a feeling I was one of the last people he'd expected to find hanging around his crime scene. His imposing presence wasn't nearly as intimidating as Logan's, but I cringed anyway.

"I have to ask, does Abigail know where you are?" He was one of the few people I knew who called Grams by her first name. Even with the dim lighting from the overhead post, I could see the flush on his cheeks, reminding me about the crush he had on my grandmother.

"No." Why would she? It wasn't like I was living at home and he'd caught me out with my friends after curfew. At least not since I'd graduated from high school.

"Mind telling me what you're doing here, then?" Roy

crossed his arms, his gaze studious.

I told him about Jessica's absence at the meeting, how I knew she was working at the cemetery, and how I'd been worried when I couldn't reach her.

"Okay, then how did you end up with Detective Prescott?" Roy tipped his head in Logan's direction.

Darn, I'd really hoped our arrival had gone unnoticed. Logan was looking our way, and I wondered if his furrowed brow was meant for Roy or me. I was leaning toward me since our first meeting had gone the opposite of well, and then there was the issue of me ignoring his instructions. "Why? What did Detective Prescott tell you?" My questions sounded more defensive than I'd wanted.

"Haven't asked him yet. Thought I'd hear what you had to say first."

"His truck got stuck, so I gave him a ride." Pesky details were such a nuisance, and I preferred to keep my explanation short. Not to mention, the less said, the less trouble I'd face later.

"Uh-huh," Roy said.

I wasn't betting, but it was a close competition between Logan and Roy as to who would win the continued scowling contest.

A flutter of movement caught my attention. Jessica had reappeared and was hovering near a police officer who was crouched not far from the spot where her body had been lying. With gloved hands, he picked up a treasure chest, then placed it in a plastic bag. Next he retrieved the coins that had spilled on the ground and dropped them into a separate bag. The chest must've been the last one Jessica was going to hide, because the only other item in the area was an empty cardboard box.

Jessica paced around the entire area before coming over to stand by me again. "Rylee, ask the sheriff if they found the map."

I made a face to let her know I had no clue what she was talking about.

"There was a master guide I used to hide the chests, and I don't see it anywhere. Please ask him if they found it."

Why would anyone want the map? The chests weren't worth a lot of money and the coins inside were fake. Knowing the location for all the hidden treasures wasn't a good enough reason for anyone to take her life. "Sheriff Dixon, did you find anything with Jessica's"—the next word was difficult and I swallowed hard to get it out—"body?"

"Like what?" There was that suspicious tone in his voice again.

"Oh, like maybe a map that shows the location for all the chests she was hiding for the treasure hunt on Saturday." Twisting my hands together nervously was not an act.

"We found a large sheet of paper, but it was smudged and covered with…" Concern glistened in his gaze.

I was certain he was going to say blood, and I was glad for Jessica's sake that he hadn't uttered it out loud.

"I'm afraid it's no longer legible and was collected as evidence," Roy continued.

Jessica sobbed. "Serena is going to be livid when she finds out the map was ruined."

"I know," I muttered.

"What do you mean, you know?" Roy eyed me suspiciously.

"I just meant it's understandable that you would keep it…as evidence."

"Okay. Stay right here, and I'll get someone to escort you out." Roy turned and walked away.

A few seconds later, Elliott headed in my direction with Logan striding next to him.

"You're not very good with instructions, are you?" Logan asked.

"I'm pretty good most of the time." I'd hoped a little humor and a smile might wear down his tough-cop routine.

"Just in case you decide to wander off again, I've asked Officer Barnes to stay with you until I'm finished."

I'd known Elliot since high school. He was a year younger and one of the sweetest guys I'd ever met. He was tall, lanky, and his uniform looked as if it was one size larger than it needed to be.

"Sorry, Rylee," Elliott said, then shyly glanced at the ground.

"It's okay." I watched Logan head back to talk with Roy.

I leaned closer to Elliott and whispered, "What's with the new detective? Since when does the sheriff bring in help from Bangor?"

"Got me, but I think Logan likes you. He hasn't stopped watching you since Roy brought you over here."

I snorted. "He's probably wondering if he saw my face on a wanted poster somewhere."

Elliott chuckled and shook his head. "Yeah, I'm sure that's it."

"So, Jessica's death wasn't an accident, was it?" I figured the best way to get more information was to start by asking simple questions.

"Nope, she was definitely murdered." Elliott hooked his thumbs on his belt.

"Told you." Jessica's voice quivered. Her hat was back to its original blue shade, and I wondered if it was the equivalent of a spiritual mood detector.

Up until now, she'd been quietly listening to our conversation. I wished there was something I could do to comfort her and draw her attention away from the scene. Frigid hugs and talking were not going to happen, not with Elliott standing here.

"Any idea what happened?" I wasn't a morbid person, but since I hadn't seen any injuries on Jessica's ghostly form, I was curious about the method used to kill her. "Do you know who did it?" I asked Elliott.

"Rylee, you know I'm not allowed to share information during an investigation."

I sighed. How exactly was I supposed to know that? It wasn't as if I spent my days hanging out at the police department or visiting crimes scenes. Other than that time when I was twelve and saw Mrs. Humphrey's cat eat Shawna's goldfish, this was my first murder. "Not even if I give you a discount on anything you want from the shop?" A discount couldn't be considered a bribe, could it?

Elliott was worse than my father when it came to anything paranormal. He came into the store weekly to see what new items had been added to the section I'd dubbed ominous.

His eyes widened, and he did a terrible job of hiding his excitement. "Well, I suppose it wouldn't hurt to share one or two details."

Logan walked up behind us, clearing his throat and glaring.

"Or not," Elliott mumbled.

"Thanks, Officer Barnes, I'll take it from here." Logan placed his hand on my elbow. "Shall we?"

Having him this close made my stomach flutter. "I suppose." I let him guide me away from the crime scene and toward the parking lot. I noticed that Jessica had done another one of her disappearing acts. So much for supernatural support.

"I don't know if it's important, but I saw Jessica arguing with a guy outside my shop this morning."

He paused for a moment. "Did you recognize him?"

"No, sorry. He was wearing a dark hoodie and I couldn't see his face."

"Thank you for the information, I'll look into it." He started walking again. "I wouldn't be doing my job if I didn't caution you to let the police handle finding your friend's killer. And that means not trying to get any more information from Officer Barnes."

My nod was simply being polite. It wasn't as if his

warning was going to deter me from finding out what had happened to Jessica. I would just need to make sure the next time I talked to Elliott that neither Roy nor Logan were anywhere nearby.

Once we reached my car, Logan braced his hand on my open door and waited for me to slide into the seat.

"Don't you need a ride?" I asked when he didn't move.

"I have a room at the inn, and the sheriff offered to give me a ride."

If he had a room, I wondered how long he'd be staying. Not that I was interested in seeing him again or anything. It was just that Jessica's murder was recent and Bangor was a few hours away. So why was he really here?

"What about your truck?" I asked.

"Already taken care of."

"If there's any damage, you can send the bill to Mysterious Baubles." I knew he was partly to blame for ending up in the ditch, but I felt guilty and wanted to do the right thing.

When he raised a questioning brow, I added, "It's my family's shop. I can give you the address if you want."

"I'm sure I can find it." He grinned. "Finding things is kind of what I do."

I remembered what he'd said to me earlier. "Does that mean I'm still a suspect?"

"I haven't decided yet." He patted the hood of my car and took a step back. "Good night, Ms. Spencer."

CHAPTER EIGHT

I'd forgotten to close the bedroom blinds the night before, and the first rays of sunlight filtered into the room. The bright warm light adamantly reminded me that I needed to get up and get ready for work. I rubbed my eyes, willing them to focus, then swung my feet over the edge of the bed.

It had been nearing midnight by the time I'd arrived home, still upset and confused about what had happened to Jessica. She was always pleasant to everyone, and I couldn't understand why anyone would want to hurt her.

The first thing I did before heading to bed was phone Jade and Shawna. Even at this late hour, they would've expected me to call, would've been angry if I hadn't. Having friends I could share my troubles with was always therapeutic. This time, though, I hadn't known where to begin or how much I wanted to tell them. It wasn't like seeing a ghost was an everyday event, and I wasn't sure how I was supposed to deal with it. I'd omitted the details about my interaction with Jessica and only told them about her death.

Sleep had come in spurts because my mind refused to shut down, too busy thinking about Jessica's demise. I hadn't seen her after leaving the cemetery. Maybe there was some supernatural rule that kept her near the place she'd been murdered.

I was desperately in need of coffee, so after a quick shower and getting dressed, I took the back stairs and headed across the street to Mattie's shop. Thankfully, she opened at seven for the townsfolk who didn't have time to prepare breakfast and needed a place to stop on their way to work. I also planned to get a muffin to replace the one I'd missed out on the day before because of Howard.

I slipped inside and took a moment to inhale the tantalizing aroma of blended coffees and delicious baked goods. As expected, the place was already busy. All the swiveling stools along the bar were occupied. Only a couple of the square tables lining the three remaining walls were empty. The low drone of human voices filled the air, and I wondered how many of the conversations centered on the news of Jessica's death.

After the next person in line grabbed their order and headed for the door, I stepped up to the counter. "Morning, Rylee. Did you want your usual?" Trina, the server working behind the counter, asked as she reached for an insulated cup and lid.

I glanced longingly at the wide variety of pastries on the shelf inside the glass case, deciding to stay with the cream cheese muffin and a French vanilla-flavored coffee. "Yes, thanks."

Trina's long blonde hair was pulled back in a ponytail and swayed back and forth as she worked. She been working part-time for the last two years. Once she graduated from high school, Mattie promoted her to full-time. Now she worked mornings and helped with the lunchtime customers. Besides making some of the best sweets in town, the place also had a great sandwich selection.

Mattie, who was working at the opposite end of the counter, tucked a loose strand of hair, more silver than blonde, behind her ear. She smiled and returned my wave, then went back to preparing a customer's order by placing items on a tray.

"That's an awful picture." I heard Jessica's disgruntled voice and tried not to act surprised or drop my coffee. Without appearing conspicuous, I shifted sideways and found her standing a foot away, hovering near a man who was sipping coffee and reading a newspaper.

Her clothes were the same, but the baseball cap was gone. Today she'd donned a straw hat with large colorful flowers adorning the wide brim. And just like the day before, her entire body was the same blue shade, while the hat and flowers glowed yellow bordering on amber.

I tossed away my theory about spirits having to remain near the place of their demise and wondered if I'd ever get used to her showing up without warning. Not that I wanted to spend the rest of my life being shadowed by her spirit. Even so, it didn't mean I wasn't going to do everything I could to help her.

With Detective Prescott viewing me as a suspect, I needed to clear my name and couldn't just wait around for the experts to do their job. I figured I was better qualified since I'd grown up in Cumberpatch and knew the town better than he did. I was also determined to find a way to remove the magic of the spirit seeker. Both items were on the top of my to-do list, right after paying for my order and easing my way through the growing crowd on my way out of the shop.

Jessica didn't seemed bothered by my hurried exit and silently moved with me to the other side of street, her movements more of a glide than a walk.

Even though I usually spent the first hour of my day catching up on bookkeeping, I wasn't in the mood to share my breakfast with Howard. I opted for avoiding the store and decided to head back to my apartment. "We can talk at my place."

I didn't know if she could move through solid objects,

so once we reached the top of the stairs, I held the door open and waited for her to go inside. I tossed my purse on the small stand next to the door and pulled two chairs away from the table in my cozy kitchen. I had a lot of questions, some of them pertaining to her ghostly abilities, some of them about her murder.

Since she'd lost her life, the normal ways of starting a conversation, such as saying "good morning," didn't seem appropriate. Neither did anything else I could come up with, so I made myself comfortable and waited for her to start talking.

Jessica stopped in front of the sofa, appearing deep in thought and staring at a blank space on the peach-colored walls of my living room. I'd made it through a sip of coffee and a bite of my muffin by the time she finally glanced in my direction.

"You have to get Barley. He's been locked up in the house all night...all alone." Jessica sobbed, the color of her hat and the flowers fading to a slate gray.

"Huh?" I coughed, nearly choking and spitting out my muffin. I didn't remember Jessica ever mentioning she had a dog before.

"Poor thing's probably frantic and wondering why I didn't come home." The more she ranted, the darker her hat got. "No one knows he's there, and if someone doesn't take care of him, he'll end up dead." Her sniffle was followed by another sob. "Like me."

A ghost crying without shedding any tears was a little unsettling. On the other hand, it came in handy when you were out of tissues.

Jessica wrung her hands together. "I know this is an inconvenience, but it's not like I asked to die yesterday." Her ghostly attempt at plopping onto the sofa lost its dramatic effect when her backside didn't even dent the cushions.

I could relate to her frustration. Being able to see a spirit and not knowing what to do about it wasn't easy either. I had no idea how to get her to the afterlife, or wherever it was spirits were supposed to go. And since I was the only one who could see her, I felt obligated to help.

I left my breakfast sitting on the table and took a seat on the cushion next to her. I couldn't offer her a comforting pat, so I clasped my hands in my lap. "Let me call Grams and tell her I'm going to be in late, then I'll see what I can do to help with Barley."

***

Jessica lived in one of the older neighborhoods in Cumberpatch Cove, where the homes ranked somewhere between extremely fancy and owned by the wealthy to slummy and soon to be condemned. The address she'd given me belonged to a single story with faded navy-blue siding trimmed in white. The lawn was a lush green, and beds of flowers lined the walkway from the sidewalk to the front porch.

As soon as I drove onto her street, my stomach experienced a nervous pang. I wondered for the fifth time since leaving my apartment if breaking into Jessica's house was such a good idea. I knew we were on a rescue mission, but this was one of those times when being helpful came with consequences. Consequences in the form of a handsome police detective who thought I was a suspect just because I'd accidentally blurted out Jessica's name.

Thinking about Logan made the knot tighten. Why couldn't I have a single thought about the man without my body reacting? Maybe my anxiety had nothing to do with Logan. Maybe I was on the verge of a panic attack.

I took several deep breaths, then glanced at Jessica. She was twisting her hands in her lap and didn't appear to be doing much better. Though I wasn't sure what she had to be worried about. If we got caught, no one would see her, and I'd be the only one getting into trouble.

"Don't park in front of my house." She pointed at an elderly woman holding a bright pink leash and standing next to a tan Chihuahua with its rear leg raised next to a sycamore tree. "That's Rita Rittleman, one of the nosiest people in the neighborhood. If she sees you near my house, she'll call the police first and ask questions later." She made a ghostly frown. "I remember this one time she reported Melinda Baker, who lives two houses down from me, for going outside in her housecoat. Rita claimed Melinda was exposing herself to everyone."

"Was she really flashing people?"

"No," Jessica harrumphed. "It was early in the morning, and she'd stepped outside to get the newspaper."

Hearing about Jessica's nosy neighbor wasn't helping the urge to circle the block and head home. I lifted my foot off the accelerator and drove five miles under the posted twenty-five-miles-per-hour speed limit. When I finally turned onto Plunder Parkway, I felt as if I'd been driving forever.

"Where do you suggest I leave my car?" I asked.

"If you drive to the next street, you can park around the corner and use the alley that runs along the back of my property."

I did as she instructed, leaving my car near the curb on an empty part of the street. After checking to make sure no one was watching, I ducked into the graveled alleyway, avoiding the occasional pothole as I followed Jessica to her home.

Her backyard had recently been mowed, the lawn surrounded by a four-foot-high white picket fence. I lifted the latch and pulled on the weathered gate. If I didn't already feel like a criminal, the hinges creaking might not have sounded so loud or caused me to cringe and grit my teeth.

"Sorry, I've been meaning to fix that," Jessica apologized, then walked through the wooden slats on the fence. I didn't know if passing through objects took practice, but for being dead less than twenty-four hours, she appeared to be adapting fairly well.

She headed straight for a concrete patio with a door centered along the house's rear wall. "I have a key hidden underneath that small pot on the left." She swept her hand toward a corner area filled with different sized pots containing various types of flowers with pink, purple, and white blossoms.

I refrained from rolling my eyes, thinking about all the murder mysteries I'd watched on television over the years. Not only was hiding a key under a pot unoriginal, it was the first place a thief or a potential killer would look. At the moment, being judgmental was moot since I preferred getting inside her house without breaking any windows and drawing the attention of her neighbors. Especially Rita, who no doubt had the police department's number on her speed dial.

I retrieved the key, did a quick trying-not-to-look-suspicious survey of the area, then unlocked the door. I turned the knob with shaky fingers, trying to justify my newly adopted life of crime by telling myself that I had permission to enter Jessica's house. Of course, if the authorities showed up, which I'd rather they didn't, I could always tell them the deceased owner had given me prior permission.

The inside of her house had a quaint and homey feel. I walked through the moderate-sized kitchen, noting the pale yellow walls and maple cabinets. A white table with matching chairs was positioned in the center of a windowed alcove on the right side of the room.

Any other time, I would have enjoyed a tour, but my racing heart made it hard to concentrate. "Which way?" I focused on getting out of the house as quickly as possible.

"Barley likes to sleep in my bedroom. It's the first door on the other side of the living room," Jessica said.

"I don't need to worry about him biting me, do I?" I was surprised that I hadn't already heard barking or growling. I wasn't an expert on pets, but Jade's mom had a miniature schnauzer, and it barked every time someone entered their house.

Visions of my worst-case scenario involved snapping teeth. My best-case scenario, some tail wagging and drooling.

"No." Jessica giggled as if I'd just asked the stupidest question ever.

Personally, I didn't see the humor. Most dogs were territorial, and I preferred not to end up with teeth marks on the fleshy part of my anatomy.

"Here, Barley," I cooed, then took a cautious step into the bedroom. A queen-size bed with a floral comforter sat in the middle of the room, an oak headboard near the far wall. Off to the left in the corner, next to a long mirrored dresser, was an oval pet bed. The fabric was a bright blue patterned with white puppy paw prints. Too bad the bed was empty and I had yet to see any sign of Jessica's pet.

"Sometimes he likes to hide under the bed." Jessica moved farther into the room.

Barley wasn't much of a guard dog, not if he was hiding under the bed. Maybe it was an animal thing, a way to lure me to his level before he pounced.

I crouched near the floor and lifted the basil-colored bed skirt. "Barley, are you under there?"

No response, no noise, no nothing. "Maybe he's hiding somewhere else." I got down on my hands and knees so I could peer under the bed. I saw movement right before I heard a growl and a creature that looked nothing like a dog shot in my direction. I screamed, scrambled backward, and pushed to my feet.

"Jessica." I slowly backed away from the fuzzy four-legged creature, a tiny gray and black-striped version of a wild cat, minus a tail and having a bad hair day. I waggled my finger. "What is that?" This was the last time I did a good deed for someone without asking *a lot* of questions first.

Jessica glared. "That's Barley. He's a Kurilian Bobtail, but he thinks he's a dog."

Okay, so Barley was a cat. A cat was doable—I hoped. If he'd been something exotic like a snake or alligator, he definitely wouldn't be leaving her house with me.

Even though Barley didn't notice that Jessica was a foot away from him, he had to be missing his owner. After sniffing my shoes, he leaned against my leg and rubbed. "Where did you get him?"

"I have an aunt who raises show cats. Barley was the runt of one of her litters and wouldn't qualify to compete, so she gave him to me."

Jessica pushed out her lower lip and eyed Barley sympathetically. "Promise me you'll give him a good home. The thought of him…"

A sobbing ghost and an adorable kitty gazing up at me expectantly while purring was more than I could handle. "I promise." I crouched beside Barley, reaching out to scratch his head. He surprised me with a gleeful meow and a jump that knocked me on the floor with him in my lap. I could do without his tiny claws kneading my leg, but I had to admit he was kind of cute, and I understood why Jessica was worried about him.

A loud chime echoed through the room, startling me and reminding me that I was somewhere I wasn't supposed to be. Who on earth would be ringing the bell to a dead person's home? I extracted Barley's nails, wrapped him in my arms, and got to my feet. Jessica gasped and vanished. No slowly fading into an evaporating mist, just poof, and she was gone.

Squirming cat in hand, I tiptoed into the living room and pressed down on a vinyl blind to make a small gap so I could see outside. Rita Rittleman was glaring at the door and impatiently jabbing the buzzer.

Had she heard my scream? Was that why she was here? "Great, now what?" I whispered to Barley, not really expecting him to answer.

I released the blind and slowly backed away from the window. There was definitely going to be a panic attack in my future if I didn't get out of the house before Rita and her nosiness decided to head to the backyard and block my only escape route.

I didn't have time to gather any of Barley's belongings, so I grabbed the blanket draped across the back of the sofa and wrapped it around him. "You need to be quiet," I murmured as I rushed through the house as quickly and silently as possible. It would take too long to return Jessica's key to its hiding spot, so I tucked it into my pocket.

Hearing the yappy barks from Rita's dog urged me into a sprint. A sprint that turned into a full-blown run once I'd cleared the gate. My heart didn't stop racing until after I'd reached my car, driven three blocks, and realized no one was following me. I glanced at Barley, who was turning the blanket into a bed on the seat next to me. "Let's never do that again, okay?"

CHAPTER NINE

So far, my attempts to be a helpful ghost whisperer had made me a semi-criminal, involved me in a near-miss escape from Rita and her yappy excuse for a dog, and left me with a new pet and no information on how to take care of him. I'd hoped Jessica would magically reappear in my car and offer me some guidance about Barley, but no such luck.

Not knowing when I'd see her next and lacking any way to summon her was frustrating. I wasn't certain if Jessica's request to give Barley a good home meant she expected him to stay with me. I intended to keep my promise to look out for him, but wasn't convinced I'd make a decent pet owner. Though the longer I was around him, the harder it was to resist those wide green eyes and furry face. It was possible that a quick search on the internet would reveal some helpful and much-needed information.

My family had never owned any pets, and stray mice didn't count, so I didn't know the first thing about taking care of one. Before heading back to the shop, I'd stopped by Purrfectly Peculiar Pets. Cassie, the helpful clerk who thought Barley was the most adorable thing she'd ever seen, supplied me with some cat care basics. After spending twenty minutes perusing the aisle filled with an ample selection of food choices, I picked two different bags of dried food shaped like fish and a variety of canned products just in case Barley was a picky eater.

I also ended up with a new fluffy black pet bed imprinted with little white dog bones and a dark blue collar with matching leash, which I immediately used to keep Barley from escaping. To make sure all his kitty needs were taken care of, my cart included a kitty litter box, a bag of litter, and two matching plastic bowls, one for water, the other for food. I really liked the set of dishes decorated with pink hearts, but decided to stick with the more masculine colors. Barley was already dealing with losing his owner. I didn't want to add to his trauma by surrounding him with a bunch of girly things.

The last thing Cassie added to my shopping bag, which wasn't on my necessity list, was a squeaky toy. The toy had been in the bottom bin near the checkout stand. While I'd been pulling things out of my shopping basket, Barley decided to sift through the colorful collection until he found a large plastic carrot with a smiling face on the side. He rolled around on the ground, toy clutched in his claws, refusing to let me take it away from him.

Forty-five minutes later, it was shortly after ten in the morning and I was pulling into the parking spot in the graveled alleyway behind Mysterious Baubles. I released a heavy sigh and stared at the gray metal door stenciled "Employees Only," trying to decide if I should take Barley up to my apartment or into the shop with me. I smiled at the way he'd buried himself underneath the blanket so all I could see was his head and the end of his tail. One look at that dark nose and twitching whiskers was all it took for me to decide I couldn't leave him alone in a place he'd never been.

I snatched the leash off the floor. "I expect you to be on your best behavior." Using the blanket to protect my clothes from his claws, I pulled him onto my lap and snapped the clasp to his collar.

After struggling with a purse that refused to stay strapped on my shoulder and the cumbersome bags of supplies, I tucked Barley against my chest because I didn't want to drag him. I'd developed a high level of respect for mothers with newborns by the time I'd made it through the back door. I stopped by the office first to drop off my purse and bags, then carried Barley into the shop.

There were a handful of customers perusing the aisles when I entered. Other than a friendly smile and one or two odd looks, nobody seemed bothered to see me carrying the fluffy furball with a leash dangling from my crossed arms. I guessed there was an advantage to selling unusual items. The little guy fit right in.

Jade was standing on a stepstool stocking a shelf, and Shawna was leaning on the display cabinet near the checkout counter. "Morning," I said, then set Barley on the floor. There was no sign of my grandmother. "Where's Grams?" I'd already called her before stopping at the pet store to let her know I was running late. I hadn't given her a reason for my delay and wasn't sure what she'd have to say about my new shop guest.

"Morning to you too," Shawna said without lifting her head from whatever article she was reading in the newspaper. "She ran across the street to see Mattie."

It always made me a little nervous when those two got together this early in the day. It usually meant they were scheming about something. Something that never boded well for me. Lately, their newest endeavor was honing their matchmaking skills with me as the intended victim.

"Have you seen this headline story about Jessica's murder?" Shawna swiped at a tear. "She was such a nice person. I can't imagine why anyone would want to hit her over the head with a shovel. This picture is awful. Why would Keith let Troy publish a crime scene photo?"

I shook my head. "Anything to sell a newspaper, I

guess." Nothing about that boy's tenacity surprised me.

I hadn't read the article yet and wasn't particularly interested in reading what Troy had to say about Jessica's death. Not after being there firsthand and getting a glimpse of Jessica's body, even if it had been covered. "By the way, did you know…"

Barley's meow made Shawna raise her head and lean farther over the counter. "What is that?"

"What is what?" Jade asked, climbing off the stool and heading in our direction.

"That." Shawna pointed at Barley.

Jade squealed and snatched him off the ground. "Aren't you just the cutest thing?" She giggled when he rubbed his nose against her neck and started to purr. "When did you decide to get a pet?"

"I didn't. He belongs…I mean, he belonged to Jessica." At the mention of her name, Jade's and Shawna's smiles disappeared, a heavy layer of melancholy instantly filling the room.

"I don't remember her mentioning anything about him yesterday." Jade eyed me curiously. She'd stopped scratching Barley's head, then started again when he persistently pawed her hand.

"Or ever, for that matter." Shawna stretched out her arms to Jade. "My turn."

"How did you know Jessica had a cat?" Jade groaned, then reluctantly handed Barley to Shawna.

"Because I told her this morning." Jessica appeared beside me. The cold brush of her arm against mine made me gasp, and I jumped. Luckily, my few backward steps ended when I bumped into the side of a shelf. At least I didn't trip and end up in a heap on the floor.

Later, when I didn't have an audience, Jessica and I were going to have a discussion about boundaries. Giving me a warning before she appeared out of nowhere was at the top of the list. I didn't know if she had the ability to move objects, but if she did, ringing a bell or making some kind of noise would be helpful.

And while we were at it, we needed to talk about the touching. As in no more, not ever.

My discomfort had completely escaped Jessica. She continued talking as if popping in whenever she wanted wasn't a big deal and hadn't almost scared the crud out of me. "I'm really sorry about ditching you after Rita rang the doorbell." She shrugged. "That woman is scary."

I rubbed my arm. "It's okay. I got out before she saw me." At least I hoped I did.

"Rylee." Jade crossed her arms and used her serious no nonsense tone. "Who are you talking to?"

I gulped, realizing my mistake. It was too late to slap a hand over my mouth or snatch back the words. My plan to resolve my ghost dilemma before anyone found out I was being haunted was officially over.

"And who didn't see you?" Shawna set Barley on the floor, moved closer to Jade and was glaring at me too.

"Rita Rittleman, my nosy neighbor who is always in everyone else's business, that's who," Jessica huffed.

Breaking up an argument between Jade and Shawna was a lot easier than having them team up and focus their attention on me. I squirmed under the scrutiny. There was no point trying to hide my new abilities from them any longer. I slumped my shoulders and grabbed the end of Barley's leash off the floor and hooked it to the nearest shelf to keep him from disappearing down an aisle.

"First of all, I may or may not have been seen by one of Jessica's neighbors when I went to her house to get Barley this morning." Before my friends had a chance to recover from their shock and close their mouths, I held up my hand to keep them from asking any questions until I'd finished. "I knew he was there because... I can see Jessica's ghost, and she told me."

Jade was the first to recover from the simultaneous, almost comical way their jaws dropped. "Are you telling us your encounter with the spirit seeker yesterday really worked?"

Shawna jerked her gaze from Jade, then returned it to me. "No way. Seriously?"

I nodded. "I'm afraid so."

"So you were talking to Jessica? She's here with us right now?" Jade asked.

"Yeah," I said.

"Sooo, does she look like a zombie?" Shawna glanced anxiously around the room.

I'd forgotten that Jade had been in the office when I'd spoken to my father about his gift. A conversation she'd shared with Shawna, if I interpreted the red blossoming on her cheeks correctly.

I couldn't believe I'd just told one of my dearest friends I could see a ghost, and all she could think about was how she looked. She was worse than my father. I ignored Jessica's confused expression. "*No*, she doesn't look like a zombie. Jessica looks like she always did." Sort of. "Only with more of a bluish glow."

"What does her head look like?" Shawna's fascination with gruesome details was a little unnerving. "Can you see…you know?" She waved her hand over her head.

"Eww, no." Although, while it didn't explain why the styles kept changing, being injured on the head might explain why she wore hats.

"Do you think she could show herself to us too?" Shawna asked.

"I have no idea." I gave Jessica a questioning glance and received a shrug. It appeared that being a new spirit didn't provide her with much information either.

"Wait, I have an idea." Jade rushed toward the back of the building, returning a few minutes later with the box containing the spirit seeker.

"What are you doing? That's dangerous, and you need to put it back." I didn't want any of my family or friends to go through what I'd experienced. Just because nothing happened to Grams when she handled the wooden cylinder didn't mean it wouldn't work on someone else. Maybe it worked like a battery and needed time to recharge.

"I would love to be able to talk to Jessica, wouldn't you?" Jade directed the question at Shawna, who was already bobbing her head. "Absolutely."

Jessica gave my friends an appreciative smile.

"Did you two miss the part where I blacked out and had a massive headache afterward? What if it does something worse to you guys?" I slapped my hands on my hips.

"I'm willing to risk it," Jade said.

"And when she's done, I want to try it too." Shawna rubbed her hands together, beaming with excitement. "I think it would be cool if all three of us could see ghosts."

Cool was not how I'd describe my newly acquired ability. I was leaning more toward problematic, frustrating, and a little creepy. "This isn't like when we were in high school and decided to get those matching fake tattoos. This won't wash off, and I don't know how to make it stop."

"I know, that's what's so awesome about it," Jade said.

Shawna widened her eyes. "Yeah, if we really could talk to ghosts, we could be famous, maybe open an investigation agency." She snapped her fingers. "Or offer our services to the bereaved and their dearly departed."

"No, we..." Before I could snatch the box out of Jade's hand, she lifted the lid and took the obelisk out of its pretty velvet bag. When nothing happened, she frowned and smacked it against her palm. "Tell me what you did to get it to work."

Relieved, yet hoping the seeker couldn't do anything worse to me, I tugged it out of Jade's hand. "It didn't come with any instructions, and I don't know how to make it work. Maybe it was a one-time thing."

My disbelief in the paranormal wavered. What if the seeker also had the ability to hand out curses? I placed it back in the chest and slammed the lid. "No one is messing around with this until I talk to Madame Minerva and find out what we're dealing with."

I set the chest on the counter, turned, crossed my arms, and refused to budge. "Do you suppose we can focus on what we need to do next to help Jessica?"

"Well, that's obvious. We need to help her move on to the afterlife," Shawna said.

Jessica had been listening intently but hadn't said anything during the entire should-we-or-shouldn't-we-use-the-seeker conversation. Everything had been stolen from her: marriage, children, growing old. Her dejected expression nearly broke my heart, and I gave her a reassuring smile. "How are we supposed to do that?" If my friends knew a way to help Jessica find peace and remove whatever voodoo the spirit seeker had stuck me with, then I was on board with the plan.

Jade leaned back against the display counter. "I think we need to find her killer."

"I totally agree. Besides, I don't think she can leave on her own." Shawna bent over to pick up a plastic bottle of herbs that Barley had batted onto the floor, then returned it to the shelf. "I may have read it somewhere, or maybe Bryce told me, but aren't spirits trapped in our realm if they have unfinished business?"

"I'd say being murdered qualifies as unfinished," Jade said.

Jessica sniffled. "You guys would really do that for me, find whoever did this and orphaned poor Barley?"

I nodded, then turned to Jade and Shawna. "Jessica doesn't know who did this to her, so what do you guys suggest we do?" Other than what I'd learned from the numerous murder mysteries I'd read and watched on television, I wasn't sure how to go about finding a killer.

Jade tapped her chin. "I think we should start by figuring out if she has any enemies." Her glance covered the area where Jessica was standing. "Can you think of anyone who would want to hurt you?"

Jessica shook her head, but I already knew the answer. "She has no clue." I tugged on Barley's leash, then pulled him into my arms before he could attack another bottle or cause any damage.

"Sometimes knowing how a person died can provide additional clues. Other than stating there was a shovel found at the scene smeared with blood, the newspaper article didn't have a lot of information." Shawna raised her brows at me. "Since you were there, care to share what you saw?"

"I'm afraid I didn't see much." Though I wondered where Troy had gotten his information about the shovel.

"Do you think whoever did this approached Jessica from behind, then hit her over the head?"

"It's possible," Shawna said.

"Well, that's just horrible," Jade exclaimed.

"Tell me about it." Jessica absently rubbed the back of her head.

Even more troubling was the possibility that whoever wielded the shovel was someone we knew, someone who lived in Cumberpatch. I scratched Barley's chin, his purrs soothing.

I'd planned to do some investigating on my own, but after hearing the gruesome details out loud, I was leery about putting my friends in danger. "Do you think we should let the police handle this?"

I received a resounding no from everyone, including Jessica.

"Oh, and speaking of law enforcement, that reminds me." Jade reached for a business card lying next to the cash register. "While you were out, a Detective Prescott stopped by. He wants you to give him a call."

I grimaced and stared at the card. This couldn't be good. "Did he say what he wanted?"

"Who cares? He's really hot, and you haven't been on a date in ages." Jade waved the thin white piece of cardboard in my face. "Maybe you should offer to give him a tour of Cumberpatch."

"I'm with Jade." Shawna grinned.

I couldn't argue either point. Logan was handsome, but after the bad way my last relationship ended, I avoided dating. "I don't need any help with my love life," I huffed.

"Yes you do, but I was thinking it would also be a good way for you to find out what information the police have on Jessica's case," Shawna said.

"In case you weren't aware, I blurted out that I knew Jessica was dead and now the detective thinks I'm a suspect."

"That's even better. It would give you an opportunity to prove that you're innocent." Jade pressed the card into my palm.

I snorted indignantly. "I *am* innocent, and I shouldn't have to prove it to anyone." At the sound of my raised voice, Barley squirmed, digging his tiny nails into my arm until I finally set him back on the floor.

"I'm just saying it would be a good way to see what he knows," Shawna said.

Even if I was interested, which I refused to admit I was, there was no way someone as good-looking as Logan would be interested in someone like me. Running the shop and having to deal with my grandmother, a new pet, and a ghost was plenty. I didn't have time to think about spending time with the handsome detective.

Besides, once he heard Grams's theories on reincarnation and learned about my father's propensity for the supernatural, crime or no crime, Detective Logan Prescott would be running away from me before I had a chance to explain.

CHAPTER TEN

Shortly before Grams returned from visiting with Mattie, I'd made Jade and Shawna promise not to tell her about my new ability to see ghosts, or at least one ghost. I hadn't seen any others, and I wanted it to stay that way. I also didn't want her to worry or call my parents. I hoped I'd be able to find a cure or some magical way to remove the power long before they returned from their cruise.

With that in mind, and Grams currently busy taking care of another customer, I headed for my office to call Madame Minerva. I smiled at Barley, who was curled up asleep on his new pet bed in the corner. He'd worn himself and me out exploring the shop. The handful of customers who'd been in and out before lunch cooed over him and laughed at his antics.

With all my failed attempts, I expected to hear the voice mail message again and nearly dropped the phone when a woman answered. "Hello, this is Madame Minerva." Her voice was deep and sounded a lot like a fake fortune-teller from a television show. Even so, I detected a hint of an accent belonging to someone who'd grown up in an East Coast state. "What can I help you with today?"

Jade walked into the room and closed the door before perching on the end of the desk.

"Uhhh." I mentally scrambled for the reason I'd called. "I recently received one of your spirit seekers as a gift, and I need…"

Madame Minerva clearly had no psychic abilities, because she interrupted me before giving me a chance to finish asking my question. "We only give refunds to the person who made the purchase." The phony accent was gone, replaced by irritation.

I took a deep breath. "I'm not interested in a refund. I want to know how long the magic lasts, or if there's a way to get rid of the powers."

"What?" she squawked.

Jade wrinkled her nose and mouthed, *What did she say?*

I shook my head, then spoke to Madame Minerva. "I got zapped by the spirit seeker you sold my father and want to know how to get rid of the powers." This time, I slowed my speech and enunciated every word.

"It really worked? You can see ghosts?" She sputtered and coughed. "I mean, of course it works." There was another long pause. "I don't know how long the magic lasts. I'm sorry you're dissatisfied with your gift, but my shop isn't responsible for the effects of the product. You'll have to refer to the warranty sheet supplied with the item."

"There was no warranty in the box. Would you be able to give me the manufacturer's information?" I asked.

She puffed out a long breath. "Look, there is no manufacturer. I found it at an estate sale, so there's nothing I can do to help you."

"Can you at least tell me…" I heard a click and rolled my eyes at the audacity of the woman to disconnect the call before I was finished. It would have been nice if I'd been able to get the name of the estate where she'd purchased the seeker. It would have given me a place to start for more information. "Well, that wasn't helpful." No doubt the woman had caller ID and wouldn't answer another call. I placed the phone back in the cradle.

Jade gripped the edge of the desk and swung her foot back and forth. "I take it you didn't find out if there was a way for anyone else to use magic either."

"I'm afraid not. Madame Minerva sounded surprised when I told her it worked." I hated dealing with suppliers who didn't stand behind the quality of their products. It sounded like Minerva, if that was even really her name, had no clue what she'd sold my father. She was nothing more than a garage sale scavenger who profited by misleading her customers and convincing them to buy other people's used items.

"Too bad. I was really hoping Shawna and I would get a chance to speak with Jessica." Jade glanced around the office. "Is she here?"

"No, she vanished about an hour ago when we started getting busy."

"Any idea where she went?" Jade asked.

I shrugged, wanting to point out that I was clueless when it came to figuring out how the spirit world worked.

The intercom on the desk phone beeped, startling both of us. "Rylee, are you there?" Grams's voice sounded from the speaker.

Jade leaned across the desk and grabbed the phone before I had a chance. "Hey, Grams. It's Jade." She bobbed her head several times. "Yeah, okay."

She wiggled her eyebrows and squirmed as if she was in desperate need of the bathroom. She covered the mouthpiece with her hand. "Oooh, it's your cute police detective."

"He's not my anything." I groaned and reluctantly held out my hand for the phone, then said, "Hello."

"Ms. Spencer, it's Detective Prescott." Even though he might have meant his deep voice to sound professional, my stomach didn't get the message and fluttered.

"Call me Rylee," I politely responded, because his continued formality was starting to annoy me.

"Rylee." He complied, but maintained a businesslike tone. "I need you to come down to the station and answer a few questions."

"Why do you need to see me? I thought I answered all your questions last night."

"I have a few more things I need to clear up."

I ignored Jade's grin. Her cheeks were so wide, she reminded me of a squirrel storing nuts for the winter. When she started making hand motions insisting that I go see Logan, I swiveled the chair and gave her my back. "You do realize I have a shop to run and can't drop everything I'm doing just because you have more questions?"

"Let me remind you this is an ongoing murder investigation. If you'd rather, I could send a patrol car to pick you up," he smugly insisted. "Or better yet, I could escort you here personally."

As much as I might enjoy the latter, I didn't want to give the gossips in town something new to talk about. If Lavender heard that I'd taken a ride in the back of a police cruiser, she'd make sure everyone thought I'd been arrested. "No, thanks to both offers. I'll stop by later this afternoon if that's okay with you."

"Fine," he answered, his voice strained. "And, *Rylee*." There was a brief pause, and I imagined him swiping his hand through his hair.

"Yes," I answered sweetly, refusing to let him believe he could intimidate me, which he could.

"Make sure you don't forget." His threat lingered in the air even after he disconnected the call.

CHAPTER ELEVEN

With very little sleep from the night before and a busy afternoon at the shop, I was exhausted by the time I got Barley settled into my apartment and then arrived in the parking lot of the Cumberpatch Cove Police Department.

Other than a middle-aged guy leaning against a chest-high counter speaking to the officer who was standing on the other side filling out paperwork, there wasn't a lot of activity in the small reception area. Judging by the man's brightly flowered shirt, khaki pants, and overhearing his loud complaint about losing his wallet, I was pretty sure he wasn't a local.

"Rylee, is everything okay?" Roy was tugging on a jacket as he entered the room from a side hallway. More than likely it was the end of his shift and he was on his way home. "Did something happen to…"

I patted his shoulder. "Don't worry, everything's fine, including Grams."

"Then what are you doing here?"

"Detective Prescott called and asked me to stop by." I left out the "insisted" part of our conversation. No need to go there unless I had to.

"My nephew did what?" Roy shook his head, then

dragged his hand down his face. "Did he bother to say why?"

Nephew? I knew the sheriff had a sister he rarely mentioned living somewhere in the state, but I'd never heard about any other family members. I was still trying to process the fact that the two were related when Logan walked into the reception area with a confident swagger.

"Because I have a few more questions about the Jessica Jenkins case."

Now that they were standing next to each other, I could see a slight resemblance around the eyes and their defined jaws. There was definitely some tension between the two men and I wondered for the second time what Logan was doing in Cumberpatch.

If he was working on Jessica's murder, it was clear he wasn't here on vacation to visit his uncle. Why was he staying at the inn instead of with Roy? Was his trip here temporary, or had he transferred? Or, and maybe this was the most plausible of my questionable theories, was he working on something in Bangor that was tied to a case here? And, if so, what did it have to do with Jessica's death?

My head was spinning with so many unanswered questions that I'd missed hearing what Logan had said. He had to clear his throat and touch my arm to get my attention. "Ms. Spencer…Rylee, I'd like you to come with me."

"Sure." I gave Roy a little wave, and since this was my first time inside the police station, I let Logan lead me farther into the building.

We walked through a wide area filled with cubicles on the left and several doors leading into offices on the right. One of the doors was closed, the name plaque engraved with Roy's title and full name.

"In here." Logan stopped at the end of the hall and opened a door to a room I assumed was used for interrogations. It was about eight by ten feet, and the white paint on the walls looked faded.

After closing the door behind us, he motioned to the chair on the opposite side of the small rectangular table sitting in the middle of the floor. "Have a seat."

I walked around the table and slid into the metal chair. It was a good thing he'd insisted I take a seat because the confidence I'd worked up on the drive over here was quickly evaporating. I kept my shaking hands clasped together in my lap underneath the table and away from his view.

He took a seat across from me, maintaining his silence as if pondering where he wanted to start. If his plan was to intimidate me, it was working. I cracked and blurted out the first thing that came to my mind. "Sooo, why didn't you tell me Roy was your uncle?"

He frowned. "I don't know you well enough to share my personal information, and you're..."

"A suspect, I know," I stated defiantly.

"As I said before, everyone is a suspect until I find out who murdered your friend." He leaned forward, bracing his elbows on the table, and steepled his fingers. "I don't believe in coincidences, especially since *our incident* occurred near the crime scene and you mentioned the victim's name *before* we reached the cemetery."

I fisted my hands. "I already told you I was going to, *not from*, the graveyard because I was worried about Jessica. So when you said someone had been killed, I *assumed* it was her."

"Yes, you did." A smile played at the corner of his lips. He straightened in his seat and crossed his arms.

This wasn't the first time since I'd met him that the humorous glint in those dark eyes was doing wispy butterfly things to my stomach. "But..." Either he didn't believe me, or there was another reason for this meeting.

"But we received a call from a concerned neighbor who reported hearing screams coming from Ms. Jenkins's home early this morning. The same neighbor also stated they saw a woman racing through the backyard." He tapped his fingers one at a time on the muscles straining beneath his light blue cotton shirt. "You wouldn't happen to know anything about that, would you?"

"Why would you think I'd know anything about it?" After years of getting into trouble with Shawna and Jade, I'd learned to pretend innocence until someone, namely one of our parents, could actually prove we were guilty.

"The description we received was of a woman with dark brown hair and about your height."

I thought I'd gotten away without being seen and silently cursed Rita Rittleman with something a little stronger than "darn." There was no point in trying to deny it. Images of being stuck in a line-up between two big hairy guys dressed in leather with tattoos covering the majority of their bodies made me rethink maintaining my silence. "Okay, I was there." I held up my hand. "But I had permission." Albeit from a ghost, but the good detective didn't need to know that important detail.

"What do you mean you had permission?" His frown was back along with his intimidating glare.

I rushed to come up with an explanation that didn't include seeing Jessica's ghost. "I was there to pick up Barley."

"Who is this Barley, and what was he doing in Ms. Jenkins's house? Because I'll need to ask him some questions too."

Good luck with that. I remembered my first encounter with the cat, then covered my mouth and coughed to stifle a giggle. Seemingly unamused, Logan frowned even more. "He's not a who. He's a what. A cat, to be more specific." I tugged on my sleeve to display the tiny scratches Barley left on my arms when I tried to take his carrot toy away from him. "Look, I have the marks to prove it."

More than anything, I wanted Logan to trust me. I remembered that I still had the key to Jessica's house, so I slipped it out of my pocket and held out my palm.

"Technically, I didn't break in. She gave me a key." I let the insinuation that I'd been given the key in case of emergencies hang in the air uncorrected.

His gaze softened but still appeared suspicious. "I'm going to assume, for now, that your visit was purely to save her pet. If I find out otherwise, answering more questions will be the least of your worries. You need to let the police handle this, which includes not bothering Officer Elliott for more information." He tapped the table with his fingertips. "Am I making myself clear?"

"Absolutely, Detective Prescott." I fought hard to keep the sarcasm out of my voice. He wasn't the one being haunted or desperately trying to find a way to help Jessica move on to the afterlife or wherever it was ghosts went when they finished their business in our world. I wasn't about to mention that my friends and I had already decided to do everything we could to find her killer. "Was there anything else?"

"Not at the moment." Logan pushed away from the table to answer a knock on the door.

After the uniformed officer mumbled something to Logan and left, he turned and said, "I have an important call. Can you find your way out on your own?"

"I think I can manage." I was already out of my seat and looking forward to getting out of this claustrophobic room. I was halfway down the hallway near the cubicles when I recognized Serena's raised voice. She stood near the doorway inside Roy's office, making me wonder if she'd arrived right after I did.

I was curious to find out what she was doing at the police station, and, lucky for me, there was a vending machine against the wall not ten feet away. I wasn't much of a soda drinker, nor was I thirsty, but it didn't stop me from digging through my purse for some change while I pretended not to listen.

"I know there's a crime scene." Serena had her back to me and tapped the floor with her foot. I didn't need to see her face to know what it looked like when she was angry. "Are you going to let the treasure hunt proceed or not?"

"Serena, a woman has lost her life." Roy's voice lacked his usual calm.

I understood his frustration. The Abbott sisters had a way of drawing out the worst emotions in people.

"Of course, I know someone has died. I'm not trying to be heartless here, but Jessica would want the Founders Day celebration to continue."

Roy appeared next to Serena, glared in my direction, then pulled the door shut and put an end to my eavesdropping.

CHAPTER TWELVE

I couldn't remember which of my friends had suggested that a visit to Jessica's crime scene after closing hours was the best way to find the clues we needed. I did know it wasn't me, and I'd voiced my concerns numerous times when they'd ambushed me after I'd returned to close the shop. Luckily, Grams had disappeared across the street to see Mattie again, so I didn't have to worry about her involvement.

After feeding Barley and making sure he had plenty of water in his bowl, I'd spent another fifteen minutes rifling through my wardrobe to find the only black outfit I owned suitable for the reconnaissance mission Jade and Shawna had dreamed up. I wasn't sure I agreed with their plan, but I couldn't come up with an alternative idea and agreed to go along to make sure they didn't get into any trouble.

It was nearing eleven at night by the time I reached Shawna and Jade's apartment. The streets had been eerily vacant, the drive taking less time than usual. My arm muscles ached, and I'd developed a twitch in several of my fingers from the death grip I'd kept on the steering wheel. To say I was worried and overly stressed about visiting the cemetery was an understatement. I wanted to help Jessica, but none of us would do her any good if we all ended up going to jail in the process.

I'd barely raised my hand to knock on their door when Jade yanked it open. "Great, you're here." She tugged the sleeve of my sweatshirt and pulled me inside, then leaned forward, turning her head to scan the sidewalk in both directions.

Did she think I was being followed? "What are you doing?"

Her cheeks flushed a rosy pink. "Nothing." She closed and locked the door, then swiped her hand through the air. "Did you bring Jessica with you?" Since I'd told her what happened when Jessica touched me, I assumed she was checking for a cold spot.

"No, but I sent her a text and told her to meet me here."

"You can do that?" Shawna walked out of the bathroom braiding her hair, then securing it with a fabric-covered tie.

I rolled my eyes and shook my head. "Sure, I have a direct link to spirit central. Anyone else you want me to call?"

"How about your great-great uncle...what's his face." Shawna scowled and flipped the braid over her shoulder. "Howard, wasn't it?"

Sometimes when I was nervous, like now, I had a tendency to be overly sarcastic. "Sorry, this whole being-able-to-talk-to-a-ghost-and-find-a-killer thing is making me a little crazy. And you know how I feel about going to the cemetery after dark." Taking a tour during the day was one thing. Visiting the resting place of the dead in the twilight hours was another. My father had dragged me on way too many ghost-hunting tours. I was sure the time I'd spent traipsing through old abandoned houses and the occasional graveyard had traumatized me plenty.

"I know, but this isn't like when we were in high school and someone..." Shawna shot Jade an accusatory glare.

"Was purposely trying to scare us."

"Don't give me that look." Jade tucked her arms across her chest. "It was all Bryce's idea."

"Sure it was." Shawna pressed her lips together tightly.

I knew better than to think Bryce had come up with the idea of terrorizing us once we got inside the graveyard all by himself. I recognized the beginnings of an argument and decided to change the subject. I walked over to the round maple laminated table in their small kitchen to examine what had been laid out for our supposed secret ops mission.

I picked up a roll of tan twine. "What's the rope for?"

"You never know what we'll find once we get there." Shawna snatched it from my hand. "Besides, the guys in my favorite television shows always have rope when they go on a mission."

"Yeah, if they're going to be scaling tall buildings." And we weren't. The cemetery had a few mausoleums, which, at most, were no bigger than an aluminum backyard tool shed. And why we'd need to climb on the roof, I had no idea.

Hanging on the back of one of the chairs was a bright lime-green backpack with a black strap and worn edges in the material along the bottom. It was the same backpack Shawna received for her twelfth birthday and had used all the way through high school. The woman saved everything. I'd bet if I looked in her bedroom closet right now, I'd find the pair of black pumps she'd worn to prom.

"I'm not sure why you bothered wearing black." I picked up the bag and swung it back and forth. "It's going to be real hard to blend in with this thing standing out like a lighthouse beacon."

Shawna snatched the bag from my hand. "Hey, that's my lucky backpack."

"It's your only backpack," Jade said.

"And your point is?" Shawna stuffed the rope into the bag, along with some bottles of water, a package of chocolate chip cookies, and three flashlights.

Jade shrugged. "No point."

"Are you two about ready to go?" It was nearing midnight and I wanted to get our excursion done and over with.

"You're not still worried about something happening during the witching hour, are you?" Jade slipped on her dark navy-blue jacket.

Yes. "No." I thought about the fluttering blue mist I'd seen the last time I was in the cemetery. What if they turned out to be more ghosts and decided I needed to be their new best friend?

***

After driving past the cemetery's main entrance and finding a secluded spot to park near the brick wall on the far side, I had a moment of déjà vu. This wasn't the first time we'd sneaked into the graveyard late at night. Getting in and out of the place was like a rite of passage for the teenagers in Cumberpatch.

Because of the town's pirate lore, some of the kids from the nearby and much smaller town of Waxford Bay included getting into our cemetery after dark on their must-do list before graduating. According to Shawna, who'd learned all kinds of gossipy details because of her job, our town's current youth still followed the old traditions.

The only thing different between now and the last time the three of us had climbed over the wall was the absence of Bryce and a couple of his friends. Back then, they hadn't been with us when we broke in, but had shown up later and done their best to scare the sugar cookies out of us. A monumental we-nearly-peed-our-pants event that he occasionally enjoyed reminding us about.

Of course, during the retelling, he forgets to include the part where I'd thrown my flashlight and nearly hit him in the head. I had poor athletic skills even then.

Once my feet were solidly planted in the lush grass, it took me a minute to get my bearings. Without the additional lights the police had set up the previous night, the interior of the cemetery appeared as creepy as I remembered it in my teens. Once I realized Jade and Shawna had started walking without me, I sucked in some air and gathered what little courage I could muster and scurried to catch up with them.

This so-called reconnaissance mission would be more successful if Jessica actually made an appearance. We needed help retracing her steps prior to her death. I'd been teasing when I said I could text her, but right now, being able to contact her would have been handy. Did ghosts have any concept of time? Could they choose to go wherever they wanted whenever they wanted, or was there some kind of spiritual intervention, something drawing the spirit to whoever could see them in this realm.

"They found her over here." I motioned toward the crime scene tape with my flashlight, half expecting to see Jessica hovering nearby.

"What about old man Anderson?" Shawna nervously glanced around. "Shouldn't we keep an eye out for him?"

I'd been so focused on how we were going to solve Jessica's murder that I'd totally forgotten about the evening groundskeeper who'd been working here for as long as I could remember.

"Probably not." Jade shrugged nonchalantly, then held up the tape so Shawna and I could scoot underneath after her. "Bryce said he usually stays in the little hut on the other side of the property most of the night watching television. His hearing's not good anymore either, so unless we make a lot of noise, he's not going to hear us."

"Do I want to know how your brother knows that?" There were quite a few things Bryce and his paranormal buddies did I was sure I didn't want to know.

There'd been rumors about Clyde drinking on the job.

Though, according to some, the problem had gotten worse after he started telling anyone who'd listen that he'd been visited by Martin Cumberpatch's ghost.

Personally, if I had to spend my nights walking around this place, I'd be hiding a bottle or two of my father's favorite whiskey in my desk and sneaking sips on a regular basis.

We didn't have to walk far before reaching the place where Jessica's body had been found.

The beam from my flashlight skimmed across the walkway, revealing a semi-rounded area where the light-colored gravel was darker than the rest.

"Is that"—Shawna paused to swallow—"her blood?"

"I think so." I shuddered, then redirected my aim to keep from staring at the spot. I didn't know what happened to crime scenes after the cops finished with them, but I hoped someone would make sure Jessica's blood was gone before allowing the tours to continue. Though I was certain some of the locals and out-of-state visitors, those with morbid curiosities, would be happy to pay extra for a viewing.

"What are we supposed to be looking for?" Shawna swung her flashlight in my direction, the light landing on my face.

I held up my hand to block the blinding beam. "How should I know? This was your idea, super sleuth."

"I know but it would be helpful if we had more information to work with. You know, like whether or not Jessica remembers seeing anyone else hanging around before she got hit over the head."

"She does know I'm standing right here and can hear everything she says, right?" Jessica asked, appearing at my side, wearing a turquoise beret.

With a noise between a gasp and a squeak, I grabbed my chest, hoping my heart wouldn't explode. "I really, really wish you'd stop doing that." I shot Jessica a sidelong glare. I knew she was a new spirit and all, but if she didn't stop showing up and jump-starting my entire system, I wasn't going to live long enough to solve her murder.

"Sorry, still working on it," Jessica said.

Right. Ghostly sincerity was hard to believe when the spirit in question was grinning at me.

"I take it Jessica finally showed up." Jade aimed her light in my direction as if catching Jessica in the beam would make her spirit magically appear.

"Good, so back to my question. Did she see anyone suspicious?" Shawna asked.

"Melissa was doing the late-afternoon tour." Jessica scrunched her nose. "I remember seeing around ten people leaving with her. Other than that, I didn't see anybody else while I was hiding the chests. Certainly no one wielding a spade."

I relayed the information. It was going to be a long, exhausting night if my friends had lots of questions. This would be so much easier if I didn't have to act as a spiritual intermediary.

"It's a little hard to solve a murder without any clues. Any suggestions where we look next?" Shawna's annoyed puff included a slump to her shoulders.

I turned to Jessica, hoping she might be able to provide an answer. She was staring at the ground, her gaze narrowed in concentration. I wasn't sure what memory she'd find in the dirt, but I held up my hand to keep Shawna and Jade from saying anything else.

It didn't take long for Jessica to smile and glance in my direction. "I'm not sure if it's important, but I remember hearing a scraping noise. Clyde mentioned he'd been having problems with pranksters. I thought the noise might be some local teens and went to investigate over there." She pointed to a path on her right. It was illuminated with in-ground lights and circled around a row of headstones, then disappeared between two mausoleums.

The special lights had been installed when someone on the city council thought it would be a good idea to include evening tours of the cemetery as part of our yearly Halloween event. The people of Cumberpatch were big on local celebrations.

"Jessica said she remembered hearing something." I turned off my flashlight and headed along the walkway with Jade, Shawna, and Jessica following closely behind me. The path curved around some headstones and stopped in front of a mausoleum.

There were two overhead fixtures attached to the underside of the roof's edge that illuminated the surname "Abbott" chiseled in large Times New Roman letters along the flat panel of the concrete in the arch above the doorway.

Shawna place one hand on her hip. "Does this mean Lavender or one of her relatives is the killer?"

"She was at the meeting with us, remember?" Jade said.

"Besides, what's her motive?" Lavender could be a pain in people's backside, mostly mine, but I had a hard time believing she was a killer. Though, at this point, I wasn't going to rule anyone out. Not until I was thoroughly convinced they had an alibi, and, in Lavender's case, a darn good one. Not that I was being petty or anything.

"You have to admit she was pretty upset when the committee outvoted her and everyone supported Jessica's idea for the treasure hunt," Jade said.

Jade made a good point. Other than Bob and a couple of other people who always went along with whatever the Abbott sisters wanted, the vote had been unanimous in favor of the hunt. I could be wrong, but I didn't think taking a hit to her social status was a good enough reason for Lavender to commit murder.

This was also the second year Cumberpatch had supported Jessica running the event. If Lavender wanted Jessica out of the way, why wait that long to do something about it? Of course, if someone wanted to commit murder and not become an immediate suspect, then waiting and biding their time would give them the perfect alibi.

"It would help if we knew the time of death." Shawna tapped her chin.

"Seriously?" Jade rolled her eyes.

"What?" Shawna dismissed her with a wave of her hand. "It's one of the first things the detectives ask the medical examiner."

I had to agree. If we knew when Jessica died, it might help eliminate some of the suspects, that was if we actually knew who the suspects were. As far as I knew, Jessica was well-liked, and other than Lavender, I couldn't think of anyone else to add to the list. "Jessica, I hate to ask, but would you mind telling us what you did all day?"

"And where you went?" Shawna interjected.

"Not at all." Jessica paced a few steps. "After I finished the late morning tour, I grabbed a sandwich from the roadside drive-through down the street, then came back here to hide the chests. I was sure I'd get them all hidden and have time to go home and change before the meeting."

I relayed what she'd said to Shawna and Jade.

"Rylee, do you think your detective friend would be willing to help out with the time thing?" Shawna said.

"I'm certain we're not friends." Not even a little, not after the warning Logan gave me during our interrogation session. I might be able to schmooze some information out of Elliott, but asking Logan could lead to handcuffs and a jail cell.

Jessica seemed to be taking the whole murder/death thing fairly well, but it didn't mean we shouldn't be aware of her feelings. I didn't want to be the one constantly reminding her that someone, possibly a person she knew, had stolen her life in a very cruel way. "Jessica, can you remember anything unusual that happened while you were hiding the chests? Something besides the weird scraping noise that would have brought you here?"

She shook her head. "Sorry, nothing."

Other than a few crickets, I didn't hear anything

unusual. In response to Jade's and Shawna's expectant looks, I said, "She remembers hearing a strange scraping noise.

"Does she remember what made the noise?" Jade asked.

Jessica shook her head.

"No, so check around and see if you can find anything that looks out of place." The area around the mausoleum was dark. I turned on my flashlight and aimed it at the ground on the right side of the concrete building. I'd gone as far as the back corner when Jade asked, "Don't they normally keep these things locked?"

If they didn't, I thought it was a good time to start, more to keep spooky dead things inside rather than giving them a chance to get out. Not sure where Jade was going with her question, I returned to the front of the building. "Why?"

"Because the lock on this one is open." Jade twisted the padlock dangling from the chain looped through the door handles.

I'd expected to see some damage, scrapes in the metal horseshoe link where someone had used a shovel to remove it from the base. I couldn't imagine either of the Abbott sisters spending any time in the crypt, let alone forgetting to secure the lock. It meant someone else with a key had entered the structure, and I wanted to know why.

"Maybe we should check inside." Jade reached for the lock.

Shawna placed a hand on Jade's forearm. "And maybe we shouldn't."

Jessica must have thought staying outside was a good idea too, because she was staring at the door and rubbing her arms.

For someone who was all about breaking into the cemetery hours earlier, Shawna seemed to have left her bravery in the car. Based on the tiny shivers creeping along my skin, my courage wasn't doing much better. The last thing I wanted to do was find another dead body. "Since we're here, we need to check it out."

Jade nodded, then unhooked the lock and pulled the chain through the thick steel rings secured to each of the doors. She leaned against the heavy metal, and after some creaking and scraping, the door slid inward.

"That's the sound I heard." Jessica's eyes went wide, her voice filled with excitement. Since pale was officially her new skin tone, I had no way of knowing if she was thrilled about going inside or worried like the rest of us.

"Jessica's sure that was the noise she heard," I said.

"Maybe someone should stay out here." Shawna crossed her arms, the beam from her flashlight flickering across her face and distorting her features. "My astrological forecast said something about avoiding dark places. I think a place filled with crawly things definitely qualifies."

I would have to see the newspaper's rendition of today's futuristic advice to believe someone on their small staff had actually printed the words "crawly things" in the daily publication. "Too bad. You wanted to search for clues, so you're going inside." I gave her my best Detective Prescott imitation. If being intimidating worked for the handsome law enforcer, I wasn't above using his technique. "Now, come on." Pretending to be in charge had its advantages. I stepped to the side and motioned for my friends to go first.

"Fine." Shawna urged Jade to go ahead of her through the opening. "But just so you know, if I die, I *am* coming back to haunt you."

"How will that be any different from what you're doing now?" Jade shrugged Shawna's hand off her arm. "You're already haunting me, and you're still alive."

"You are not..." Shawna froze, her shriek deafening. All I could see from where I was standing was a streak of black skittering across the floor, followed by an echoing squeak. I hoped Bryce had been right and Clyde had passed out from one too many drinks, because there was no way he didn't hear my friend's hysterics.

I relaxed the death grip I had on the collar of my jacket and bravely took a step around her. I aimed my light at the corner and caught a pair of beady eyes in the beam. A pair of eyes that transformed into a small furry creature that squeaked several more times before squeezing through a large crack running from the floor halfway up the wall. "Shawna, it's only a mouse." The mouse looked an awful lot like Howard, same beady stare, same pink feet, same pink tail. Since I wasn't a rodent expert, I brushed it off as a coincidence.

"Yeah, a mouse the size of a Saint Bernard."

Jade aimed her flashlight at the spot where the wall met the ceiling in one corner of the room. "Next you'll be telling me the spider on that web is the size of a bat and can fly."

"What spider? Where?" Shawna's voice rose an octave higher, and she latched onto my arm, her grip as tight as a metal vise.

Jade laughed and jiggled the light across the empty web.

"Sooo not funny," Shawna harrumphed and walked toward the center of the room, nervously glancing between the floor and the walls lined with name plates of Serena and Lavender's deceased ancestors.

All I could say was Jade better sleep with one eye open tonight just in case Shawna decided to get even.

CHAPTER THIRTEEN

I was ready to admit that searching the crypt for clues was a complete failure. While Shawna and Jade were busy tormenting each other, I gave the interior of the room one last sweep with the beam from my flashlight and caught a glint of gold on the floor. I glanced warily at the crack in the wall in case Shawna's furry friend decided to return before I knelt to investigate.

The shiny object turned out to be a coin. It looked a lot like the replicated doubloons from the chests I'd purchased for the treasure hunt, so I assumed Jessica had been carrying a chest when she was searching for the source of the noise. I checked the rest of the floor, expecting to find more coins or the chest they'd fallen out of, but didn't find anything. Why there was only one coin in the room was a mystery I didn't get a chance to solve.

Jessica had opted to remain near the entryway without coming inside, so when she called my name, it echoed through the small enclosure. "Rylee," she repeated when I didn't answer immediately. This time, her voice was louder and laced with panic.

I slipped the coin into my pants pocket. "Jessica, is everything okay?" My expedient efforts to leave the room ended the huffy standoff between Shawna and Jade. They rushed to follow me outside.

"I thought I heard something." Jessica stared at the darkened shadows on the other side of the building, the edges of her beret a yellowy orange.

Between the noise from the door and Shawna's shriek, I wouldn't be surprised if we'd managed to wake a few of the deceased residents. I quickly scanned the area, searching for signs of fluttering blue mist, and was relieved when I didn't see any. It was most likely Clyde, but after experiencing the weirdest two days of my life, which included standing here conversing with a ghost, I was willing to believe anything was possible.

"What's wrong with Jessica? Did she see something?" Jade snapped her head back and forth, scanning the area around the nearby headstones.

"She thought she heard a noise." I tipped my chin in the same direction Jessica was staring. "It could be Clyde making his rounds." I wasn't totally convinced, and neither were Jade and Shawna, who were now huddling next to me.

"Why don't you ask her to go check it out? It's not like whatever is out there can hurt her," Shawna said.

Jade flicked Shawna's arm. "Geez, that's not very sensitive."

"What? I know you both were thinking it." Shawna leaned closer and whispered, "Sorry, Jessica."

"It doesn't matter," I whispered back. "She vanished again, so we're on our own."

The three-quarter moon, concealed earlier by a cluster of clouds, peeked from beneath the billowy edges, illuminated the graveyard, making it possible to see the surrounding row of graves without using our flashlights. It also exposed a man wearing a dark hoodie and trying to hide by pressing his body against the side of the second mausoleum down from us.

Seeing a Howard look-alike inside the crypt was one

thing, but seeing someone wearing a similar hoodie to the guy I'd seen bothering Jessica outside the shop the day before wasn't a coincidence. "Hey, you!" I hollered and started walking toward him, which prompted the guy to take off running.

Jade grabbed my sleeve. "Rylee, are you crazy? Where do you think you're going?"

"To get some answers." I wanted to know who this guy was and why he was here. Did he have his own agenda, or had he been following us?

"What if he's Jessica's killer?" Jade asked.

"Good point. Let's follow him, find out where he's going, then call the sheriff." I reached for the cell in my pocket.

"I have a better idea." Shawna bolted past Jade and me.

"She's not going to…" I couldn't believe the friend who'd been scared to enter the mausoleum moments ago was now chasing after a potential murderer.

"Yep," Jade called over her shoulder, already running after Shawna. Her bouncing bright green backpack was the last glimpse I got of her before she disappeared between some buildings on our left.

I shook my head and forced my short legs to move before my brain had a chance to tell me how stupid it was to chase someone I didn't know, someone who was bigger than me…someone who might be a murderer.

Jade's designer boots weren't ideal for running, and it didn't take me long to catch up with her. The guy, however, had the advantage by being a good foot taller with longer legs, and easily put distance between us. I thought for sure we were going to lose him until Shawna came barreling back into view.

"Got ya," she yelled, then leaped onto his back, wrapping herself around his body as if she were a monkey and he was her favorite tree.

"Get her off me." The guy spun in a circle, flailing his arms and trying to dislodge her. He tripped and fell to the ground with Shawna still clinging to his back and straddling his waist. It was a good thing she'd tackled him in an area covered with freshly mowed grass and not a walkway; otherwise, he'd have ended up with a mouth full of dirt and gravel.

A few seconds later, Jade and I skidded to a stop close to them. I bent forward, my free hand pressed against my abdomen as I tried to catch my breath. "Shawna." I gulped more air. "What the heck are you doing? You need to get off him."

Determination flared in Shawna's steely gaze, and she clamped her knees tighter against his ribs. "Not until he tells us who he is and why he was spying on us."

Astonished and never having witnessed the ninja wrestler side of my friend, all I could do was stand there and shake my head. If this guy really was the killer, I was more than happy to let Shawna keep him pinned down until we got answers and waited for the police. Before making the call, I needed to come up with a reasonable explanation why the three of us had been all over Logan's crime scene after his earlier warning to stay away.

Jade eased a few steps closer to Shawna. "Nate, is that you?" She bent down and pulled the hood off his head, exposing the rest of his face. "What are you doing here?"

"Wait, you know this guy?" I pursed my lips, confused.

"Yeah he's…"

"With us." Hearing a man's voice made me jump and spin.

If I'd known karate, which luckily for Bryce I didn't, he'd have seen some serious moves. I lowered my flashlight and waited for Myra Mitchell, one of the members of his club, and him to get closer.

"Not cool, Bryce." Jade chastised her brother, then smiled at Myra. "Hey, Myra."

Myra acknowledged Jade's greeting with a nod and a grunt. I'd only met Myra a couple of times. She stood a few inches taller than me, had hair the color of a dull strawberry, lacked a sense of humor, and never smiled. She was also an avid paranormal geek, maybe even worse than Bryce, though nowhere near the enthusiast that my father was.

"Sorry, Sis. Didn't mean to scare you." Bryce nodded at Jade and held his hand out to Shawna, who reluctantly removed herself from Nate's back.

"Thanks." Nate got to his feet and dusted dirt from the front of his now-grass-stained pants. His brown eyes were a few shades darker than his hair. Some of the lengths had escaped from the tie at his nape and draped his shoulders. "Who's the crazy lady?" His glare never left Shawna.

"I'm Jade's roommate, and I'm not *crazy*." Shawna fisted her hands and returned Nate's stare as if daring him to make a wrong move so she could tackle him again.

Doing my usual intervention thing, I turned to Bryce. "I saw Nate arguing with Jessica yesterday outside my shop." I tapped my flashlight against my palm. "Care to tell us what that was all about and why you followed us here?"

"Whoa." Nate took a step back and waved his hand wildly through the air. "I didn't kill her if that's what you're thinking. I would never hurt Jessica." He choked on a sob. "We broke up a couple of months ago, and I was trying to get back together with her."

"If that's true, then why were you spying on us?" Though Nate seemed genuinely upset about Jessica's death, I wasn't ready to exclude him as a suspect.

"We thought you might need our help now that you can see ghosts." Bryce beamed.

I snapped my attention to Jade, who sheepishly shrugged, then glared at her brother. I knew I should have included all family members when I made Shawna and her swear not to tell Grams about my ability. Or better yet, I should have insisted on a blood oath, which in our case was a solemn pledge, a joining of pin-pricked fingertips.

I blew out an exasperated sigh, my silent glare a

promise that Jade could expect retribution for blabbing to her brother. Though in her defense, she didn't stand a chance against her brother's skills of persuasion. He'd been practicing on the three of us for years. He was like an annoying miniature dog nipping at someone's heels if he got the slightest inkling they might be keeping a secret from him. If convincing someone to give him the information he wanted didn't work, he resorted to bribery, and I wondered what he'd promised his sister in return for telling him about my new ability.

"First of all, it's ghost singular, not plural," I corrected Bryce's assumption. "And we don't need your help."

Speaking of said ghost, Jessica picked that moment to appear next to me. "Sorry, I bailed. Sometimes when I get scared, I… Hey." She pointed at Bryce, but her attention was focused on Nate. "What are they doing here?"

Now that the ghost was out of the bag, so to speak, I didn't think there was any reason to pretend I couldn't see or hear her. "Supposedly, they are under the impression that we need their help." As soon as I said the words, everyone stopped what they were doing to look at me.

"Is Jessica here…now?" Nate sounded hopeful.

I nodded.

"Can you…I mean…can she hear me?" he asked.

"Yes, she…"

"Oh, come on." Myra clenched her fists and glanced around the group. "You guys don't really believe she can talk to ghosts, do you?" She shot her suspicious squint in my direction. "Anyone can pretend to talk to thin air. It doesn't mean she can actually speak to spirits."

"I don't care if you believe her or not." Shawna draped her arm across my shoulder. "We didn't ask for your help, so feel free to leave."

"Shawna, I'm sure Myra didn't mean it." Bryce's plea to stay on Shawna's good side went unanswered.

"I told you I'd find them." My grandmother's all too familiar booming voice filled the air.

I groaned and watched Mattie and Grams, their flashlight beams bouncing off several headstones, approaching our group as if they were important speakers about to address a special audience. Grams's presentation would have been more believable if she hadn't been wearing a hot-pink sweatsuit haphazardly tucked into a pair of men's high-top boots.

Since the only pair of boots my father owned were made for cold weather, and I'd never seen my grandfather wearing anything that closely resembled Grams's footwear when he was alive, I wondered if she'd borrowed them from Mattie's nephew.

I didn't know Josh well and had only met him a couple of times when he'd come to Cumberpatch to visit his aunt. I got the impression he was a bit of a slob. His entire wardrobe consisted of wrinkled shirts and jeans with holes that looked as if he'd taken a scissor to them himself. No doubt expecting to make some kind of fashion statement.

Mattie's attire wasn't much better, but at least her clothes were a dark navy-blue and blended more with the surroundings. She didn't stand out like a lighthouse beacon, not like my grandmother did.

"Grams, what are you doing here?" I really wanted to know who was responsible for sending out the let's-meet-at-the-graveyard-for-a-party memo.

At this rate, it was only a matter of time before the cops made an appearance and hauled us to jail. Thinking about Logan's warning and knowing we were going to get caught only made my slowly growing headache worse. I didn't know how I was going to explain my way out of this massive debacle. Not only had I disobeyed an officer of the law, I had way too many accomplices. All I could see was an image of him wearing an I-told-you-so smirk as he slapped a pair of handcuffs on my wrists.

"You didn't think we were going to let you have all the fun, did you?" Grams turned off her light.

"Fun… How…" I turned to Jade. "Did you…?" I

wasn't happy that she'd blabbed to her brother, but I understood it. My grandmother finding out about our reconnaissance mission, not so much. Especially since we'd all sworn an oath of secrecy to keep her from finding out. Jade slowly shook her head back and forth, so I shifted my annoyed glare at Shawna, who mouthed, *No way*.

"The girls didn't say anything about you being able to see Jessica's ghost, though they should have." The look Grams gave Jade and Shawna had them both cowering and scooting closer to me. Sometimes my grandmother could be scary.

I refused to be intimidated. "Then how did you find out?"

Grams grinned and wiggled her brows. "Oh, a little mouse told me."

At least she hadn't told everyone that *the mouse* was my great-great uncle Howard, so that was a plus.

"Does this mean you're here to help too?" Shawna asked.

"Yes." Grams beamed with enthusiasm. "Did you find out anything, maybe uncover some riveting clues?"

I nudged Shawna and groaned. Other than his professed love for Jessica, I didn't know anything about Nate, which made him a possible suspect. Until I was certain I could cross him off the list, I wasn't going to share the information my friends and I had gathered so far.

"I'll tell you about it later." I turned to Jade and Shawna for support. "I think we've done enough investigating for tonight and should head home."

"Or we could regroup at the clubhouse." Bryce could win awards for his tenacity.

"Do you really think that's a good idea?" Myra, who'd been eying me with a skeptical frown since Bryce made introductions, crossed her arms defiantly. I expected her to break out in a temper tantrum any minute. "They aren't members, and we have, you know, confidential stuff."

Unless one of them was a vampire or witch disguised as a geek—extremely unlikely—I couldn't fathom what kind of information they had that she thought required secrecy, and honestly, I didn't want to know.

"Don't worry, Myra, our secrets are safe. I… What's that noise?" Bryce turned toward the sound of an engine's rumble.

"It has to be Clyde making his rounds. The township got him a refurbished golf cart after he complained about his gout acting up," Jessica said, then disappeared.

"Jessica thinks it's Clyde." I turned to address the group and discovered everyone except me had decided it was time to leave.

"Rylee, come on." Jade had reached the yellow strip of tape and was motioning for me to move.

With the engine getting louder and the threat of being caught bearing down on me, I ran faster than I'd ever run before.

CHAPTER FOURTEEN

"Thank you so much. My niece is going to love these."
A middle-aged woman with wire-rimmed glasses and
wearing a peach-colored T-shirt with a basket of kittens
printed on the front tucked her wallet back into her purse.

The steady routine of taking care of customers made
the morning pass swiftly, but it didn't keep my mind off
our failed attempt to solve Jessica's murder. The only thing
the trip to the cemetery the night before had gained me
was the possibility that the Abbott sisters might be
involved, and maybe Nate too.

I didn't know if Jessica being on the Founders Day
committee had anything to do with her murder, but I
figured I should consider all the members suspect until I
got a chance to rule them out.

"Glad to hear it." I picked up the bag containing a
book on the history of Cumberpatch and two on the
basics of witchcraft, then handed it to her.

As soon as she walked away, Barley jumped up on the
counter, meowed, and rubbed against my arm. "Is this
what you're looking for?" I giggled, then scratched behind
his ears.

It had taken less than twenty-four hours for the furry

feline to make himself at home. Not only had he purred his way into the hearts of my friends, he'd wrapped my grandmother around his paw and was now the shop's official new mascot. No matter how many of the items I had to restock on the lower shelves after he'd been exploring and playing, finding him a new home was not an option.

Howard seemed undaunted by having a cat on the premises. I was certain his random appearances in my office were motivated by hopes that I would leave another muffin unattended. I still couldn't believe Barley hadn't tried to eat him during their first encounter.

The bell above the door tinkled, and Lavender swept into the shop as if she was late for an appointment. She marched past Jade, who was filling a bin with toy pirate sabers, and headed straight toward me. Barley hissed, jumped to the floor, and disappeared down the back hallway before she made it halfway across the shop.

With a frustrated grunt, Lavender dropped the cardboard box she'd been carrying onto the counter, making a heavy thump.

"Good morning, Lavender. Is there a problem?" I hoped whatever was in the box wasn't going to become my newest annoyance.

"Yes, there's a problem," she snapped. "Without Jessica, the committee is shorthanded. I already had plenty of things to do before Saturday." She opened the box and pulled out a thick stack of brochures secured with a rubber band around the center. "Now I'm stuck finishing the rest of her tasks, which includes delivering these to all the committee members." She slapped the stack in front of me.

I ran my finger along the top of the colorful pamphlet. I'd seen the draft copy before they'd been sent to the printers and knew the inside and back page announced the events taking place during the Founders Day celebration. All the shop owners were supposed to hand them out for the rest of the week. A similar pamphlet, one that resembled a treasure map, wouldn't be handed out until the beginning of the hunt and only to those who were paying to participate.

"Wow, are those the new brochures?" Jade walked around the counter to stand next to me. She slipped the top copy out from beneath the band, then opened it to see the information inside. "Jessica made a good choice when she hired the Fussy Flair Print Shop. They always do a great job."

No sooner had Jade mentioned her name than Jessica appeared on her other side and leaned over her shoulder to get a better look at her handiwork. It was the second day in a row for the cute turquoise beret she was wearing.

Jade must have gotten a chill, because she set the paper down and briskly rubbed her arm, then glanced at me. I interpreted her wrinkled nose as a way of asking if Jessica was standing next to her, and gave her a brief nod.

Seeing Jessica and the brochures at the same time gave me an idea, a way to work through the suspects I'd generated after last night's graveyard fiasco, many of whom were on the Founders Day committee. "Lavender, if it would help, I'd be happy to deliver the pamphlets to the shop owners on Swashbuckler." It was the perfect way to narrow down my list.

"I don't know." Lavender tapped her nails on the counter, making a production of pondering my request.

I presented her with a friendly smile, hoping it would reassure her enough to entrust me with the assignment.

"I suppose that would be all right." She pushed the box closer to me, sounding as if she'd just bestowed me with a great honor.

I refrained from rolling my eyes and latched on to the cardboard container before she changed her mind.

Grams walked into the shop from the back area, cuddling Barley against her chest and petting him. She'd barely taken two steps into the room when the cat perked its ears and growled at Lavender. "Smart kitty," Grams mumbled loud enough for Lavender to hear. "Maybe she's the one who offed your previous owner so she could be in charge of next year's activities."

Lavender gasped, her face turning a bright red.

Even though my friends and I had already discussed our thoughts about Lavender having something to do with Jessica's death, I didn't think my grandmother should be voicing it out loud. "Grams," I said, shooting her a scathing look.

"Rylee, make sure you deliver all of these *today.*" Lavender sneered in Grams's direction, then turned and walked away, slamming the door upon her exit.

"She is nothing but nasty to you, so why did you offer to help?" Grams set Barley on the floor, then walked around to the front of the counter. "It's not like you owe her any favors and don't have plenty to do around here."

Jade shifted sideways and propped an elbow on the counter. "I wouldn't mind hearing the reason for that myself."

After last night, there was no point in trying to keep things from my grandmother. "I thought it would be a good way to get alibis from the other committee members without anyone getting suspicious."

"That's actually a great idea." Grams beamed at me proudly.

"Jessica's here, so I'll take her with me," I said.

Jade grinned. "Even better."

The bell tinkled again, and Shawna entered, wearing her cantina uniform. She was closely followed by a family with two small boys. Not surprisingly, the young ones headed straight for the bin of pirate toys closest to the door. Telling Jessica she'd have to be a silent partner so people wouldn't think I was talking to myself would have to wait until later.

"Hey everyone, what's up?" Shawna reached for the newspaper she had tucked under her arm as she strolled along the aisle leading toward our group.

After she placed the paper on the counter, Jade handed her one of the Founders Day brochures. "Riley's going to do some recon, and I'll fill you in later." She moved in the direction of the new customers.

"Oh, okay." Shawna's confusion lasted as long as it took her to snatch Barley from Grams.

"I guess I'll see you later." I reached for the box, motioned for Jessica to follow me, then headed for the door.

CHAPTER FIFTEEN

Four shops and two eating establishments later, my list of suspects was considerably smaller, but I wasn't any closer to finding out who might have wanted to hurt Jessica. Everyone I'd talked to so far was fond of her and seemed to have a reasonable alibi. The day of her murder, they'd either been working or spending time with their family prior to attending the committee meeting.

Jessica had been popping in and out for the last hour and a half. I assumed hearing how upset and shocked people were about her death was difficult, so when she didn't offer an explanation about leaving, I didn't ask for one. I also wasn't going to wait for her to return before continuing on with my mission.

I opened the door for Barnacle Bob's Bookstore and walked inside, the brass bell above my head tinkling. I took a few seconds to let my eyes adjust to the dimly lit interior, then glanced around. On my right and going all the way to the back of the shop were shelves nearly reaching the ceiling. At the end of each shelf was a large printed sign listing the type of books stocked in each section. The room was quiet, and I didn't see any customers but that didn't mean there weren't any perusing the aisles outside my view.

To my left, I found Bob perched on a stool behind a long wooden counter. There was a cash register sitting on one end, and on the other was a small twirling stand displaying an assortment of colorful bookmarks ranging from cute animals to anything related to pirates.

Bob jerked his head in my direction, his pale cheeks flushing red. "Rylee." He slammed the book he was reading shut, then walked around to my side of the counter.

I caught a glimpse of the words "Rare Coins" in bright yellow letters in the title and asked, "Are you a collector?" Because of our town's history, coin collecting was a popular hobby among some of the locals, and it wouldn't surprise me if he was one of them.

"Nah, just curious. The book was a special customer order, but they never showed to pick it up." He tugged on the collar of his blue-and-yellow-plaid shirt. "I guess it will be a new addition for my pirate lore section."

I reached around him and picked up the book, then leafed through it, taking note of the photos of numerous coins with their values listed below the pictures. "Lyle would've loved this." His death weighed heavily on my mind, so it was no surprise that seeing the book reminded me of him. During several of the discussions we'd shared about the coins in the museum, he'd mentioned being a collector.

Bob snatched the book from my hands. "Was there something I could help you with, a particular book you were looking for?" His tone was terse, and he shifted nervously from one foot to the other.

"Actually, I'm here on committee business." Instead of toting the cardboard box filled with brochures that Lavender left at the shop, I'd used the largest shopping bag I could find with our store's logo printed on the plastic. Since I was going to be out and mingling with potential customers, it never hurt to do some advertising. I reached into my bag and pulled out a stack of brochures and handed it to him.

"Oh, okay, thanks." I thought it was strange that he set them on the counter without bothering to look at them.

"I still can't believe what happened to Jessica, how someone could do that to her."

"Yes, a real shame." Bob swiped his hand over his bald head.

"Oh, did you know her well?" I asked, hoping to lead the conversation to the day of Jessica's murder.

"Only from the committee." He slid past me and moved to the other side of the counter again. "I really don't have time for any more questions, so if you'll excuse me, I have a lot of work to do."

There still hadn't been any customers leaving or entering his store. People reacted differently to the death of someone they knew. I got the feeling I'd touched a nerve when I'd mentioned Lyle, but his reaction when I'd mentioned Jessica was worse. I got the impression that if Bob could've shoved me out of his shop without being rude, he would have. "Sure, no problem." I turned and made my way to the door.

Once outside, I stopped to pause. Visiting business owners and asking questions to determine alibis or to find out if anyone had a grudge against Jessica had turned out to be a lot of work. I had several more shops to visit, but my encounter with Bob left me emotionally drained, and in need of a break.

Thanks to the thoughtful members of the Cumberpatch Cove city council, almost every block along the boulevard had at least one wooden bench trimmed with black wrought iron sitting next to a building and bolted to the sidewalk. Not only were they a convenient place to relax, but they provided a great view of the activity along the street. Luckily, I didn't have to go far to find an unoccupied seat.

I'd only been sitting a few minutes when I felt a

familiar chill and Jessica appeared beside me. "Did you find out anything useful?"

I pulled my cell out of my pocket and placed it next to my ear and pretended to be on a call so I could talk freely to Jessica without anyone thinking I was nuts. "This is harder than my busiest day at work." I'd been using the ingenious plan to communicate with her since leaving the shop, and it appeared to be working.

Several small groups of tourists walked by, some pausing briefly to look in the storefront windows of each shop they passed, others busily chatting. Even Troy, who was probably on his way to interview someone for an article in the newspaper, whisked past me with a curt nod and wave.

"You aren't going to stop helping me, are you?" Jessica fidgeted with the shimmering fabric of her skirt. "Because I really don't want to be stuck like this forever."

I had no way of knowing whether or not finding her killer would help her move on, but it wasn't going to keep me from trying. "No, I'm going to do everything I can to help you. You know that goes for Shawna, Jade, and Grams too, right?"

"I know, and I really appreciate it, Rylee." Her attempt at a half smile saddened me. "I also wanted to thank you for adopting Barley. I know he's not an ideal pet, but I do appreciate everything you've done for him."

"It's really no…" I had a perfect view of the other side of the street, and all thoughts of what I was going to say disappeared when I saw Logan leaving the pirate museum. It was a good thing people were milling about; otherwise, he might have caught me staring with a little admiration thrown in for good measure.

It was purely from an investigative standpoint, not because the casual pants he was wearing showed off his backside. I watched him walk to the next block and was glad to see his truck was no longer in the ditch. I was even happier to see him drive away.

"No, what?" Jessica glanced in the direction I was staring. "Hey, isn't that the detective who was at the crime scene? Do you think he knows something?"

"Yes to your first question and maybe to your second." Curiosity got the better of me, and instead of heading into the last store on this side of the street, I decided to make a detour to the museum first. "Come on, let's go talk to Greg." I got to my feet, tucked the cell in my back pocket, then reached for the bag of brochures sitting under the bench.

"Okay," Jessica said without an argument and followed me across the street.

Besides the adjoining parking lot, which lacked any empty spaces, the building housing the museum took up nearly an entire block. I walked into the lobby with Jessica gliding in behind me and was unable to miss the Founders Day exhibit Serena had asked about during the last committee meeting.

The entire board was filled with a huge rendition of the pirate, Martin Cumberpatch. He was holding an ancient map with a classic "X" near the bottom to mark the spot where a treasure could be found. The wording along the top of the board was similar to the information on the brochures. It listed Saturday's events, including the morning parade, a children's carnival, and the afternoon hunt at the cemetery. The large open treasure chest filled with fake coins sitting on the floor in front of the display was a nice touch.

Off to the left, there was a new person, a middle-aged man I didn't recognize, taking tickets and preparing to give a guided tour through the pirate exhibition section. I was reminded of Lyle's death, and a heaviness settled in my chest. It was so hard to believe he'd been involved with the robbery at the museum in Bangor. He'd always been proud of our town's history and took great care of the collection of articles from our town's past.

"Hey, Rylee." Greg's greeting pulled me back to the

present. "I'll be right with you." He was standing behind a display counter, placing some recently purchased souvenirs in a bag for a customer. He'd made quite a few improvements to the museum in the two years he'd been in Cumberpatch. Besides the admission he charged to view the roped-off part of the museum, he made additional income from the gift shop designed to look like the deck of a pirate ship that he'd added near the entrance. From what I'd heard, his business was doing well.

I left Jessica appreciatively admiring the cardboard display—a result of her handiwork—and placed my bag on the counter next to Greg.

"What can I do for you?" He smiled, pouring on his businesslike charm. "I'm assuming you didn't stop by for a tour."

"No." I opened the bag and pulled out two of the rubber-banded stacks and set them on the counter. "Lavender needed help, so I brought you some of the Founders Day brochures to hand out to customers."

"I still can't believe what happened to Jessica. It was horrible." He glanced remorsefully at the pamphlets, then back to me. "I really liked her. She had some great marketing ideas."

"Yeah, not that it did me much good," Jessica mumbled. She hadn't moved, but I could see her from where I was standing. She'd been listening to our conversation and glanced in our direction when she heard her name.

Until I could prove that Greg really did have car trouble before the meeting, I didn't have a strong enough alibi to remove him from my list. Since he'd shown up at the cemetery shortly after I did, there was no point asking him the same questions I'd asked the other members on the committee. Instead, I jumped right to the reason that prompted me to skip the other shops and come here in the first place. "Wasn't that Detective Prescott I saw leaving a few minutes ago?"

"Yes, he said he was questioning anyone who knew Jessica, specifically everyone who worked with her on the committee." Greg removed the bands and placed the brochures in a neat stack next to his cash register. "I doubt I was much help." He tapped the counter. "Other than talking to her at the meetings, I didn't know her that well."

Greg wasn't the only one who didn't know much about Jessica. She hadn't grown up in Cumberpatch, and I'd only met her a year ago when my mother volunteered me to work on the committee. If we met on the street our visits were no more than short friendly chats, which was why I hadn't known anything about her past relationship with Nate or that she had a pet cat.

"So far, he's telling the truth," Jessica interjected while maintaining her vigil near the display.

Since all Greg's current customers were on the tour and no one was standing around to overhear our conversation, I decided to broaden my investigation to include the unanswered questions I had about Lyle's death. "I didn't get the chance to mention it the other night, but I was sorry to hear about Lyle."

"Me too. He was a good employee, great with the customers, and hard to replace," Greg said.

I leaned on the edge of the counter. "Any idea what he was doing in Bangor?"

"Only what I read in the newspaper."

"If he did steal the coins, I wonder what happened to them," I speculated, then shifted the strap of my purse farther up my shoulder.

"I guess we'll never know." Greg swept his hand through his hair, glancing anxiously to the area where the tour would end.

"Did he say or do anything before he left for Bangor? Anything that made you think he was having some kind of trouble?" It was going to take more than supposition and a newspaper article to convince me of Lyle's involvement.

I knew money was a major reason people ended up

turning to crime. Was it possible that Lyle had found himself in a bad financial situation?

"Not that I noticed. He said he needed a few days off to handle some personal issues." Greg's tone sharpened with irritation, an indication he was reaching the end of his question threshold.

It didn't stop me from persisting. "Any idea what those issues might have been?"

So far, the things I knew about Lyle's death didn't make any sense. I couldn't dismiss the notion that there was a connection between what happened to Jessica and him. There wasn't anything physical that tied them together, rather a gut reaction, a feeling the two events were somehow linked. No matter what I did, I couldn't shake the overwhelming notion that I was on to something.

Greg crossed his arms and furrowed his brows. "What's this all about? Why all the questions?"

I'm trying to solve a murder, maybe two. "I'm sorry, I didn't mean to sound pushy. It's just that I knew Lyle a long time...since high school. I guess I'm having a hard time believing he was a thief and was looking for some closure." Pretending to be sincere wasn't one of my better skills, and I hoped he'd believe my attempt to be genuinely concerned. "I thought since you worked with him every day that maybe..."

"Look, I get it, and I wish I could help, but Lyle never told me why he needed the time off." Greg backed away from the counter.

The tour had ended, and people were filtering into the shop, putting an end to our conversation. "Well, it looks like you're going to be busy." I grabbed my bag and slipped it over my arm. "If you run out of brochures, please let me know."

"I will, and thanks." He patted the stack, then dismissed me to help a customer.

Unease clung to my chest tighter than the humid air

that wrapped itself around me the second I opened the door. I retrieved my phone and held it against my ear so I could speak to Jessica. "Did you get the feeling he was hiding something?"

"I'm not sure." She paced alongside me. "He seemed okay until you started talking about Lyle."

"That's what I thought too." I headed for the nearest street crosswalk.

"So why were you questioning him about Lyle?" Jessica turned to face me while we waited for the light to change.

I took a moment to consider whether or not I wanted to share my theory with her. It wasn't as if she'd be able to repeat anything I told her. It also couldn't hurt to get someone else's insight. Not that I didn't want to hear Jade's and Shawna's opinions, which at this point would be skeptical. I wanted to have more information before I said anything to them. I also didn't want my theories to reach Grams. There was no telling what kind of bizarre scheme she'd come up with if she thought I was right.

Once we reached the other side of the street, I kept my phone in place and slowed to an easy stroll. "I know it might sound crazy, but I think there's a connection between Lyle's death and what happened to you."

Jessica scrunched her nose. "That's kind of a stretch, don't you think?"

"Maybe, but I find it strange that a detective from Bangor shows up right after their museum is robbed, the same day something happens to you." Granted, with Logan being Roy's nephew, he could just be here to help with Jessica's murder investigation, but somehow I didn't think so. "Greg said Logan told him he was questioning all the members on the committee, so why did he head back to his truck instead of visiting some of the other shops? Surely someone would have mentioned it when I was dropping off the brochures." Being questioned by an out-of-town detective was something the gossips wouldn't resist sharing.

"Oh." Jessica widened her eyes, her gaze shooting across the street, then back to me. "You might be right. It does seem strange that the detective's only stop was the museum."

"Exactly." I gave her a satisfied grin. Maybe my intuition was doing a better job than I thought.

Feeling better about my decision to do some further digging into Lyle's death, I glanced to my left and realized that we'd stopped in front of the last shop on my list. I'd been dreading going into Classic Broom ever since I agreed to help Lavender. I wasn't bothered by the store as much as I was about speaking with Edith and Joyce Haverston. The sisters were personable, even polite. It was how perceptive they were, how they knew personal things about people, things no one else knew.

"Do *you* really have to go in there?" Jessica warily took a gliding step backward.

What happened to we? "Yes." I figured I was on my own, expecting her to disappear any second, and reached for the brass door handle. As ominous as the wooden door appeared with its intricately carved store's name and a witch flying on a broom right beneath it, it didn't stop the tourists and many of the locals from entering the shop.

Once the bell stopped tinkling and the door closed with a hard click behind me, I swallowed back my fear and moved farther into the shop.

"Rylee, it's so good to see you." Edith stepped away from a shelf and swept across the floor, her black skirt billowing around her ankles. She'd used combs adorned with a side view of a raven, its wings spread wide and a shiny red jewel for its eye, to pull her long blonde hair away from both sides of her face.

"Yes indeed." Joyce appeared on my left in the entry of a hall leading to the back of the shop. Her crystal-blue eyes, a matching set to her sister's, sparkled with excitement. "What can we do for you?"

"I'm delivering the brochures for Saturday." I glanced

from one sister to the other.

"Oooh, let me see." Joyce held out her hand and wiggled her fingers like a child expecting candy.

I reached into the plastic bag and removed two of the last three bound stacks, handing one to each of them.

Joyce pulled a pamphlet free, tucked the remainder under her arm, then unfolded the colorfully printed paper. Edith moved closer, hovering over Joyce's shoulder while they examined one side, then the other.

"Marsha always does such a lovely job," Joyce cooed, then refolded the brochure and placed the stack on a nearby display counter containing shelves of various-sized colored bottles, the wording on the labels ranging from love potions to wart removal.

The Marsha she mentioned was the owner of the Fussy Flair Print Shop and had the best reputation in town for designing and print reproductions.

"We'll miss Jessica dearly, but I was glad to hear the sheriff came to his senses and decided to let the Founders Day celebration continue," Edith said.

I didn't mention that I thought the browbeating I'd overheard Serena give Roy might have had a lot to do with his decision.

"Rumor has it that his nephew is visiting from Bangor and helping with the case." Joyce gave Edith a knowing wink.

"Logan, I mean Detective Prescott, hasn't been by to question you, has he?" It never hurt to verify my assumption that Logan was in Cumberpatch because his investigation had something to do with Lyle's death.

"Not yet, but we expect him to arrive no later than tomorrow." Edith smiled at Joyce, who concurred with her prediction by giving her sister a nod.

"How? Why?" I wasn't ready to give up on my theory and groaned.

"To ask us about Lyle, of course." Edith patted my arm in a motherly fashion. "Not that we have any idea what he was doing in Bangor."

"No, no idea." Joyce tapped her chin. "Although, he did seem pretty upset about something when I ran into him coming out of the bookstore a few days before his..." She whispered the word "death."

Now that I thought about it, Bob's behavior had been a little strange when I picked up that book on coins and mentioned Lyle. Had something happened between them, some kind of argument? Was Lyle the customer who had ordered the book? And if he was, why didn't Bob want me to know?

"Rylee." Joyce's voice pulled me from my thoughts. "In case you were wondering, the shop was busy that afternoon, and we were both here working until we left for the meeting."

"How did you..." Her intuition was unnerving. I played with the edge of my plastic bag.

Edith studied me with her narrowed gaze. "There's something different about you." She swirled her hand through the air. "Possibly a new gift with spiritual-seeking abilities." Edith glanced at Joyce. "Wouldn't you agree?"

Joyce stepped a little closer, scrutinizing me from top to bottom. "Most definitely, and newly acquired would be my guess."

I snapped my gaping jaw closed before speaking. "You know about my...that I can see Jessica?"

"Of course," Edith and Joyce replied in unison.

"Do you also know how I can get rid of it, the power, I mean?" I hadn't planned to stop helping Jessica, but I didn't want unsolicited visits by other spirits to be a part of my future either.

Edith furrowed her brows. "It's possible, but why would you want to give up something so wonderful?"

I wouldn't exactly call it wonderful or even pleasant. Seeing a ghost was changing my life, and not necessarily for the better.

When I didn't answer, Joyce said, "Why don't you tell

us how you gained the ability."

I spent the next few minutes explaining everything I knew about the spirit seeker, from the inscription inside the box to the way I'd been zapped unconscious and woken up by Grams. I left out my father's expectation of seeing zombies, but did include Madame Minerva's slip about finding it at a yard sale.

"Unbelievable," Edith gasped.

"I'm not making this up," I huffed.

Joyce squeezed my arm. "Oh, we believe you. My sister is upset that someone would be so irresponsible and leave a magical item lying around for anyone to find. Can you imagine what would have happened if a child had gotten a hold of it?"

That horrible thought hadn't occurred to me and wasn't something I wanted to dwell on.

"On the other hand, it is fortuitous that your father sent it to you." Edith smiled.

I didn't see anything positive about the whole situation, and shook my head. "Why is that?"

"Your years of skepticism make you the perfect candidate to receive the power," Joyce said.

"Perfect…what? I don't understand." My disbelief in the paranormal wasn't something I shared outside of my family and close friends. I wondered, once again, how often my father conversed with the sisters.

"Because you did not covet the magic, you will not take it for granted, therefore making you…" Joyce swept her hand through the air.

"An exquisite recipient," Edith finished for her.

"Okaaay." I drew out the word. "Does that mean there's a way to return the gift to the seeker?" If it was possible to put the magic back, I'd toss the obelisk, box and all, into the sea where no one would ever find it.

"I've never heard of a way to return the powers to an object once they've been released." Joyce pressed her lips together tightly.

Edith sighed. "Neither have I."

"Are you sure?" I hated sounding as desperate as I felt. "Is it possible to do some research, maybe check with your...friends?" I'd been about to say coven and caught myself.

After my recent experience with the ghostly realm, the existence of a witching community in or near Cumberpatch was definitely more believable. Not that it meant the Haverston sisters were upstanding members of that kind of organization.

Joyce gave me an empathetic look and glanced at Edith. "I suppose it wouldn't hurt to check."

"I agree, but the chances are extremely high that it can't be undone," Edith said.

"Although"—Joyce rubbed her chin—"there is the possibility this is a one-time occurrence."

"What does that mean?" I tried not to sound too hopeful.

"In some cases, the magic is focused on helping one spirit," Joyce said. "Once Jessica is released from this world..."

"The magic will disperse," Edith and Joyce said together, then grinned.

The sisters and their antics were starting to grow on me and my trepidation about coming into the shop dwindled even more. "So how do I release Jessica?" The sooner I helped her into the afterlife, the sooner I could get back to my semi-normal life.

"By finding her peace," Joyce said.

"In other words, I need to find her killer." Jade and Shawna would be happy to know they were right.

They nodded, then Joyce frowned and held up her hand. "And quickly, because some magic comes with a time restraint."

"A what?" I asked.

"What my sister is trying to say..." Edith scrunched her nose at Joyce. "There is the possibility that the longer it takes for Jessica to find resolution, the harder it will be for her to move on."

I tucked my hair behind my ear. "So you're saying if no one figures out who did this to her, she'll be stuck here forever?" Great. Like I really needed the added pressure of a spiritual clock doing a countdown and threatening to leave me with a ghost companion for the rest of my life. I shook my head and groaned. "How much time does Jessica have?"

Edith gave me a sympathetic pat. "Since we don't know the extent of the seeker's magic, I'd say you have a week, two at the most."

In other words, I didn't have any time to waste. "I don't suppose you have any ideas about who might have done this, do you?"

Edith shrugged. "I'm afraid not."

I gave them an it-was-worth-a-try look. I'd stayed longer than expected and shifted toward the door. "Thank you for your help, but I should get going."

"Stop by anytime." Joyce walked along with me, then held the door as I stepped outside.

"I will." I'd only made it a few steps when Edith peeked around her sister. "Rylee, one more thing."

I stopped and glanced over my shoulder. "Yes?"

"Trust a relative to give you the signs." She winked and followed Joyce back inside before I could ask who she was talking about.

I stared at the carving on the closed door as if the witch would suddenly come to life and explain Edith's words of advice. Grams was the only relative in town at the moment. Did it mean my grandmother was going to have another one of her dreams and provide me with insight to helping Jessica?

"What was Edith talking about?" I noticed Jessica standing near the building, impressed that her anxiety about going into the Classic Broom hadn't induced another disappearing act.

"I'm not sure, but they were convinced that the only way to help you move on is to find the person who…you know." Using the word murdered or killed seemed insensitive, so I refrained.

"The sisters are pretty insightful. Did they have any thoughts on who might have done it?" Jessica asked.

"No, and after talking to them, I think we can remove them from our suspect list."

"Wait a second." Jessica reached for me, her hand passing through my arm, a chill skittering across my skin. "I've seen that guy before."

I ignored the shiver and the urge to rub my arm. "Which guy?"

"That one over there." She pointed across the street.

The tourist Greg and I had chatted with when I was waiting for Logan at the crime scene was coming out of the museum. I was about to tell her that she'd seen me talking to him at the cemetery, then remembered it was during the time she'd done one of her disappearing acts.

"Excuse me." A woman in her forties, fighting with three large shopping bags and dragging a child who clearly wanted to be somewhere else, sidestepped around me.

"Sorry." I hadn't realized I'd stopped in the middle of the sidewalk and was getting more than one disapproving glare from the people passing. I moved out of the way and leaned against the building with my phone pressed to my ear. I waited for another couple to pass, then spoke to Jessica. "Where do you remember seeing him?"

"He took my late-morning tour the day I…" Jessica made a slicing motion across her neck.

Her attempt at humor seemed a little morbid, but who was I to judge? I was more interested in the new bit of information she'd given me about the overly friendly tourist guy. When I'd spoken to him the other evening, he'd made it sound like he'd never been on a tour. He'd thought the crime scene was part of a mystery event. Why had he lied? Until now, the idea of someone from out of town being a suspect hadn't even occurred to me.

I thought about following him to see where he went, but quickly dismissed the idea when he crossed the street and entered the bookstore. I really didn't have any reason to be suspicious of him. He wasn't acting any different than any of the other tourists that visited our town. I might be curious about his reasons for being less than truthful, but it wasn't enough to turn me into a stalker. At least not yet, not until I'd had a chance to talk to Jade and Shawna about my murder connection theory.

I glanced in Jessica's direction, then pushed away from the building. "Come on, let's head back to the shop."

CHAPTER SIXTEEN

Normally, relaxing in the sanctuary of my cozy apartment was easy. Tonight, however, the less than helpful information I'd gathered during my mediocre sleuthing expedition had left me tense and in need of something to help with my mounting headache. Barley didn't seem to have a problem with the relaxation thing. He was comfortably sprawled on my cushioned chair between my thigh and the armrest.

Jade and Shawna were sitting on the sofa opposite me with paper plates containing partially eaten slices of cheese and pepperoni pizza on their laps. Since we didn't want a surprise visit from Bryce and his paranormal followers, we decided to meet at my place after the shop closed for the day.

I also didn't want my grandmother to get involved. Luckily, she was with Mattie at their monthly movie night and would be preoccupied at the local theater for a couple of hours.

I finished the last of my pizza and waited for my friends to digest the brief recap I'd given them about everyone I'd visited, including details about the conversations I'd had with Bob, Greg, and the Haverston sisters. I ended by sharing my speculations about the mysterious guy from the cemetery.

"Do you think we should tell your cute detective about the tourist guy?" Jade asked.

Logan wasn't my cute anything, and my friends constantly reminding me about his good looks was annoying. I held my tongue because arguing would only encourage my friends to push the conversation toward the matchmaker path I wanted to avoid. "Tell him what exactly? That I can talk to Jessica's ghost and she remembers seeing the guy on her tour the day she died?" I placed my elbows on my knees and propped my head in my hands. "Oh yeah, that sounds believable."

Shawna stopped midbite. "I still can't believe Logan is Roy's nephew. I knew the sheriff had a sister who moved away years ago, but he never mentioned any other relatives."

"If you're not going to tell the detective about the tourist guy, are you at least going to take my advice and ask him out?" Jade asked.

I rolled my eyes. "Dating. You want me to think about dating at a time like this?"

"I was talking about getting information for us on the case." Jade bobbed her head. "But dating would be good. It's been over a year since you broke it off with what's his name."

Hudson Bradley. My friends knew better than to mention the disloyal, cheating jerk's name out loud. I'd devoted almost two years to a relationship I thought was going to last forever. Until I found out his idea of commitment meant seeing a woman who lived in Waxford Bay at the same time he was seeing me.

When my father heard that Hudson had broken my heart—juicy tidbits traveled faster than lightning in Cumberpatch—he offered to search the Internet to find someone to curse him. Though I readily declined, it was one of those rare times when I loved my father and his paranormal obsession. If Hudson hadn't moved to take a job in Portland shortly after we broke up, I might have changed my mind.

"The last time I spoke with Logan he was pretty clear he didn't want me to do any investigating." I slumped back in my chair. "I don't think any amount of prying is going to get us the information we need."

Logan's previous lecture about letting local law enforcement handle the investigation rang through my mind. I planned to spare myself any further grief and placed asking him questions at the bottom of my last-resort list.

Jade's smirk had me holding up my hand. "And absolutely no dating."

Her shrug meant we'd be revisiting the topic again later.

"Speaking of suspects, was Jessica able to remember anything else?" Shawna asked. "Anyone that seemed suspicious to her?"

I glanced around the room, checking to see if she'd made an appearance. "I haven't seen her since late this afternoon when I told her I was heading back to the shop." Jessica hadn't seemed upset or startled, so I had no clue why she disappeared.

"There is something else I want to run by you guys to see what you think." I reached next to me and scratched Barley behind the ears. His ensuing purr didn't hinder his ability to keep his green eyes focused on the last two remaining pepperoni-and-cheese-smothered slices left in the cardboard box sitting on top of the coffee table inches away from us.

"Let's have it." Shawna leaned forward and snagged her fourth slice of pizza.

I didn't have my friend's metabolism, and two pieces was my limit. I set my paper plate on the table next to the box. "I think there might be a connection between Lyle's and Jessica's deaths." When I didn't get the skeptical eye rolls I'd expected, I spent the next few minutes explaining my theories and everything I'd learned about Lyle so far.

Jade slipped off her heels and tucked her feet to the side on the cushion next to her. "Since we all agree that Lyle could be innocent, we need to find out why someone would want to kill him."

I was glad my friends didn't think I was nuts and adored them for their support more in that moment than I had in all the years I'd known them.

"And Jessica." Shawna snaked her tongue out to catch a string of cheese hanging off her pizza.

The action drew Barley's attention, and he abandoned me in favor of rubbing against Shawna's legs, his gaze never leaving her food. I grinned. His secret wish for a piece of meat to roll off her slice and land on the floor wasn't going to come true.

"Don't forget, whoever is behind this went to a lot of trouble to make it look like Lyle was responsible for the theft." Until someone proved me wrong, I refused to believe he was a thief.

"Do we think Lyle was in the wrong place at the wrong time?" Shawna cleaned her fingers with a napkin, then crumpled it and set it on the stack of discarded plates on the table.

"Is it possible he knew the thief and somehow found out about the theft?" Jade snatched Barley off the floor and placed him on her lap.

"If he did, then why go all the way to Bangor? Why not just call Roy?" I asked.

"Maybe he discovered something but couldn't prove it and was afraid the police wouldn't believe him," Shawna said.

"If that's the case, then how do we figure out what he knew?" Jade scratched Barley's head until he started purring.

I rubbed my chin. "That's a darn good question."

CHAPTER SEVENTEEN

It was already Friday, the air was filled with a current of excitement, and the day passed in a flurry of activity. All the store owners on Swashbuckler, myself included, had spent the day preparing for the weekend's events. The Saturday-afternoon treasure hunt was the most popular topic of conversation in my family's shop. It was all the tourists could talk about, that and the possibility of seeing a real live crime scene. It was morbid to think about, but Jessica's death caused a considerable boost to the Cumberpatch economy. In all the years I'd lived here, all twenty-eight of them, I'd never seen such a large influx of visitors for the Founders Day event before.

As much as I needed a relaxing and fun-filled night out with my friends, time for Jessica was running out. I couldn't stop thinking about Lyle and hoping he'd found a way to pass over to the spiritual beyond, and focused on finding a way to solve their murders. Shawna and Jade had left shortly after helping me close the store with plans to head over to the Shivering Timbers Saloon and a promise to check in with me later.

Instead of going upstairs to my apartment, I'd stayed behind to finish up some paperwork. After that, I'd spent an additional hour going through any information I could find on the Internet about the theft at the Bangor museum, searching for even the smallest clue that would help me with my sleuthing endeavors. All the articles I read contained similar versions of the same information, nothing new or useful.

With my head propped on my hands, I sat at my desk and stared at the unwrapped paper containing a ham and cheese on whole wheat sitting in front of me. Somehow the appetite I'd had for the meal I'd purchased from Mattie's had vanished somewhere on the street between her shop and mine.

If the police, or rather Logan, had solved the crime, the locals would have been buzzing with the information. Since that hadn't happened and what little information I had wasn't enough to solve the case, I was dealing with the realization I might never be able to help Jessica's ghost find resolution to her death.

At least I wasn't alone in my suffering. Barley and Howard were on my desk, the cat sprawled across some files, the mouse sitting near the edge. Their newly formed friendship wasn't any odder than the rest of my current yet strange reality, so I had no problem accepting it.

Neither of them appeared particularly happy. Who could blame them? If the mouse really was my reincarnated relative, though I still had doubts, a lot of them, he'd failed to complete his mission. Poor Barley had to be suffering from some transitional aftereffects. He'd lost his owner and gone from living in a large house to a small apartment.

We were all in need of a little comfort, so I unwrapped the sandwich and tore off two strips of ham and placed a piece in front of each of them. It might not be a good idea to add table scraps to Barley's diet, but he didn't seem to mind and quickly devoured the meat.

Things were going fine with the group commiseration until my so-called great-great uncle got greedy and tried to snatch the next scrap I'd placed in front of Barley. After a kitty growl and Howard's squeak of defiance, my desk turned into a flurry of flying papers, paws, and fur.

The papers took flight, swirling through the air like mini tornadoes. The treasure chest Jessica had given me bounced against the wall and flipped on its side. Howard, followed closely by Barley, sailed off the desk. The coins spilled from inside the box, some of them forming a pile of gold near my computer screen while others rolled across the desk's surface before plummeting over the edge.

"Rylee." Jessica magically appeared, her trilling voice adding to the chaos.

I gasped, flinging the sandwich, the soft bread and contents splatting against the wall, then dropping to the floor. Howard, followed by Barley, made one lap around my legs before disappearing into the small gap between the wall and the filing cabinet. Barley, content that he won the round, headed for the spare pet bed I kept in the corner. After a long stretch and a few paw flexes, he curled up in the middle of the soft fabric.

Jessica grinned, oblivious to the havoc going on around her. "You'll never guess what happened."

Besides my near miss with a heart attack? It was hard to keep from yelling at her for scaring me when it was the first time she'd been this excited since the night of her demise. "Where have you been?" I tried not to sound like a scolding mother.

"I've been following Scott since I left you yesterday."

I didn't know anybody named Scott and wondered who she'd been tailing. I kept from overreacting by reminding myself that she could follow whoever she wanted because no one else could see her. Was it possible for ghosts to get dementia from being in the human realm too long? And if so, why hadn't the Haverston sisters bothered to mention the side effect? "Who's Scott?"

"The tourist guy that took my tour." She clapped her hands together.

I was surprised at Jessica's ingenuity. "How did you find out his name?" I leaned over and scooped up the now ruined sandwich, then wiped the gob of mayonnaise off the floor before dumping everything in the trash.

"He's staying at the inn, and that's what I overheard Lavender call him." Jessica smiled, proud of the tidbit she'd obtained. "Hey, being a ghost has some benefits."

I crossed my arms and sat on the edge of the desk. "Did you find out anything helpful during your sleuthing expedition?"

Jessica grinned. "Only that I think you're right."

"Oh yeah, right about what?" She and I had discussed several things over the past couple of days, and I hoped the information was related to her murder.

"About there being a connection between the break-in at the museum and what happened to Lyle and me."

"What makes you say that?" I asked, eager to hear what she'd learned.

"I also heard Scott tell one of the other guests he was from Bangor."

"Hmmm." I tapped my chin. "That can't be a coincidence."

Jessica finally took the time to glance around the room and noticed the mess on my desk. She looked at me as if I were the worst housekeeper ever. "What happened in here?"

"Food disagreement." I tipped my head toward Barley, who was innocently pretending he had nothing to do with the condition of my office.

"I'm so sorry." Covering her mouth and giggling wasn't a good way to convince me she was being sincere.

Since I was the one who had to clean up the disaster, I didn't find it amusing. "Back to me being right." I got down on my knees, figuring I could clean and listen to what she had to say at the same time. I scooped up the coins that had fallen on the floor.

"After Scott stopped by his room at the inn, he left his

rental car parked on a side street, then inside the cemetery," Jessica said.

My curiosity was piqued, so I sat back on my haunches and gave her my full attention.

"He waited for the final tour to end and everyone to leave, then headed for the Abbott mausoleum." Jessica was practically floating with glee.

"He did?" Personally, I was shocked and clamped my gaping jaw.

"Yes, and remember how Jade found the lock on the outside door open?"

I nodded.

"Someone locked it after we left the other night, but Scott was able to get inside with his own key." Jessica slapped her hands on her hips. "Does that mean he's the one who did this to me?" The slight shimmer on her cheeks glowed brighter.

"It's obvious he's working with someone local. It's the only way he could've gotten a key." It was a helpful clue, a connection we needed, just not enough to solve the case. "It doesn't necessarily mean he's the one who...you know." Was Scott the killer, the one responsible for Lyle's and Jessica's deaths? Was it the person he was working with, or were they both responsible?

I had too many unanswered questions and not enough answers.

First I needed to do something about the dejected look on Jessica's face. "Do you think it's possible Scott knows Clyde?"

She shook her head. "I don't think so. I'm good with faces, and up until a few days ago, I'd never seen him hanging around the cemetery before."

I couldn't remember seeing him in Cumberpatch before either. Maybe Scott had a close friend or a relative, someone who made a trip to visit him wherever he lived. At the moment, I'd bet it was Bangor.

"What about Lavender and Serena? Scott is staying at

the inn, and the crypt does belong to them. Do you think they could be involved?"

"The Abbott sisters can be a royal pain in everyone's backside, but I find it hard to believe they're criminal masterminds." It didn't mean I was going to cross them off the suspect list, not until I knew for sure.

Jessica sighed. "You're probably right."

Finding out more about Scott moved to the top of my to-do list. There was also the question of where he got the key and why he needed to get into the mausoleum in the first place. More importantly, I wanted to know whether or not he had anything to do with Jessica's death. "What did Scott do once he went inside the crypt?"

"It looked like he was searching for something on the floor, and when he couldn't find it, he started cursing."

I glanced at the fake coins I was clutching, then ran a fingertip over the stamped surface of one of them. My mind finally clicked on what had been bothering me about the coin I'd found, and I knew immediately why Scott had returned to the graveyard.

"I don't believe it." I jumped to my feet and reached for the jacket I'd hung on a hook behind the door. I'd been so busy trying to find Jessica's killer, I'd forgotten that I'd stuck the coin in my pocket. "He must have been looking for this. I found it the other night when we were searching for clues."

Jessica eased closer. "That looks real."

"At the time, I thought it fell out of one of your treasure chests." Now that I could see the coin under better lighting, and after doing a quick comparison with the fake versions scattered on my desk, I was certain it was authentic.

Finding the coin didn't prove that Lyle wasn't a thief, only that he wasn't the one who'd dropped it in the crypt. Once again, I was wondering what was so important about the Abbott mausoleum and what it had to do with the coin theft.

"Do you think it's one of the Bangor coins?" she asked.

"Wait a second." I dug through the stack of old newspapers Grams kept in a box on the floor in the corner for future recycling or whenever she needed to wrap something breakable. A quarter of the way through the stack, I found what I was looking for.

I spread the newspaper on the desk and pointed at the headline article for the Bangor Museum theft. "I knew it." Next to the portrait of Lyle was a picture of a doubloon. A doubloon that looked exactly like the one I was holding and worth thousands of dollars. "This is one of the stolen doubloons!"

Jessica widened her eyes. "So what are we going to do now?"

I did what I always did in situations like this when I didn't have a good answer. I picked up my cell and, with a shaking hand, selected one of the three top autodial numbers. "Call for reinforcements."

CHAPTER EIGHTEEN

Jade and Shawna weren't too happy about having their fun night out cut short, not until I told them about Scott. They hadn't bothered to go home and change before showing up an hour later dressed in short skirts and heels. Jade's slim-fitting dress was a shade of teal, her favorite color. The majority of Shawna's outfit was black, accented with a purple that matched the new streaks in her hair.

After calling my friends, I'd gone to the twenty-four hour gas/grocery store a few blocks away and picked up an assortment of snacks. "Help yourselves." I pointed at the coffee table covered with food, knowing it wouldn't take my friends long to slip off their heels and situate themselves comfortably on the sofa. I took my usual spot in the chair across from them and was joined by Barley a few minutes later.

"Bryce isn't going to be happy when he finds out why we ditched him." Jade grabbed a plate, then filled it with two kinds of chips and a chocolate cookie.

"You didn't tell him you were coming here, did you?" Bryce by himself I could handle, but if he did make an appearance, I didn't think he'd be alone. The last thing I wanted was his paranormal squad showing up and asking a bunch of questions. Myra already thought I was a fraud, and I preferred not to spend the rest of my night trying to convince her differently.

Shawna scooped some dip with a chip and paused before taking a bite. "No way."

"Someone"—Jade shot a sidelong glance at Shawna—"told him they'd seen Martin Cumberpatch's ghost, so he was too busy checking out the bar when we left."

"Hey, you said we needed to find a way to leave without hurting his feelings or letting him know where we were going. Besides, I said it was a rumor, not an actual fact." Shawna chomped on another chip. "I'm not responsible if your brother *assumed* there'd been a spirit sighting."

I clamped my lips together to keep from grinning. Sometimes Jade forgot that Shawna took whatever she was told literally, a fact she constantly proved with her mischievous behavior. "Thanks for helping out."

"Not a problem." Shawna dropped another handful of chips on her plate, then settled back into the cushions. "Is Jessica here so we can ask her questions and get more details about this Scott character?"

"No, she said she wanted to do some more sleuthing."

"Meaning?" Jade asked.

"She went to find Scott and follow him around some more." I caught Barley's paw before he could snag a chip off my plate.

"Do you think he'll lead her to his accomplice?" Jade held a dip-laden chip near her mouth.

"Maybe, but doubtful." I thought about all the people who'd visited the shop over the last couple of days and how they couldn't stop talking about the murder and planned to visit the crime scene. "With all the attention Jessica's death is getting, he'll probably want to keep a low profile."

I remembered my first encounter with Scott at the cemetery. He'd shown up right after Greg had arrived. I already knew his curious tourist routine had been an act, confirmed by Jessica when she told me he'd been on her tour. The two men hadn't seemed to know each other, but what if they did? What if them both being in the graveyard at the same time hadn't been a coincidence? What if the car trouble Greg said made him late for the committee meeting hadn't really happened? What if he'd been the one responsible for Jessica's demise?

The thought of Greg being a killer made me nauseous. Until I had answers to my questions and figured out why he'd been acting so funny during our last visit, he'd remain on my suspect list.

"Makes sense." Shawna bobbed her head. "Do you think it's time to share what we know with Roy?"

"Or his nephew?" Jade shot a grin in my direction.

When it came to matchmaking, Jade's persistence was worse than her brother's. "If the doubloon I have was stolen from the museum, do you think Logan will simply believe I found it? I can't tell him about Scott without explaining Jessica's part in obtaining the information. There's no way he's going to believe me. And since he already thinks Lyle was involved with the theft, he'll more than likely think I was his accomplice."

The knock on the door startled me and had me rushing to answer to tell Bryce he needed to go home.

I barely got the door open when Grams grinned and swept into the room carrying two six-packs of wine coolers, one containing watermelon-flavored drinks, the other a citrus blend. "Hey, girls." She set the cardboard carriers on the table between the bags of chips, then plopped on the couch between Shawna and Jade. "What did I miss?"

At least the worn jeans and button-down shirt she was wearing were more stylish and suitable for an evening out, nothing like the blaring hot pink she'd worn to the cemetery.

"Oooh, Abby, you're the best." Shawna leaned forward

and grabbed one of the bottles filled with an orange liquid.

"Ditto." Jade smiled and reached for her own bottle.

"Grams, it's always nice to see you, but what are you doing here?" I couldn't resist taking a watermelon cooler and unscrewing the cap as I returned to my seat.

"Did you really think I wasn't going to help you find Jessica's killer?" She twisted the cap off her drink and took a swig.

"I guess not." Although a granddaughter could hope.

"Tell me everything, and don't leave out any details," Grams insisted.

I used the next few minutes to fill her in on the information I'd gathered so far, including what Jessica had found out about Scott.

"Interesting." Grams snagged a cookie and a handful of chips. One of the chips missed her plate and landed on the floor near Shawna's feet.

Barley sprang from the chair, reaching the chip before Grams did. After scarfing it down with a few crunchy chews, he remained seated, tail swishing and gaze alert, watching for the next escaping morsel.

"Last night, Mattie and I coaxed Roy into joining us for movie night," Grams said.

Since Roy'd had a thing for Grams for years, I doubt she had to do much coaxing.

"And?" Jade shifted sideways, giving my grandmother her full attention.

"Afterward, we took him to the ice cream shop, and he had two scoops of raspberry ice cream smothered with chocolate syrup, which, if you didn't know, is his favorite."

I didn't know, wasn't sure why I should care, and wanted to know what it had to do with what we were discussing. "Grams." I tipped my head, giving her one of my get-to-the-point looks.

She took a bite of her cookie, then slowly chewed and swallowed, a blatant attempt to build everyone's anticipation.

Unlike me, who'd gotten the full dose of her ploys since the age of nine, my friends eagerly and patiently waited for her to continue. This was one of those times when I was glad I hadn't inherited the melodramatic gene that ran on her side of the family.

"According to Roy, they still don't know who was responsible for Jessica's death," Grams said.

"Did he mention whether or not they had any suspects?" Shawna placed her bottle on the coffee table, then leaned forward to pull Barley into her lap.

"He refused to…" It was hard not to giggle when Grams acted like a teenager and made air quotes with her fingers, "…divulge what he considered official police information. We did, however, spend some time talking about that gorgeous nephew of his." Her smirk was directed at me. "Logan is definitely investigating Lyle's death and the break-in at the museum. I also found out there have been similar thefts at other museums along the coast in the last six months, and the police think they are all connected."

I held back on joining her playfulness with a fist pump and shouting *I knew it*. Instead, I asked, "If there was more than one theft, doesn't that prove Lyle wasn't involved?"

"Maybe so, but we still don't know who the killer or killers are." Grams reached for another cooler.

"Or what was so important about using the Abbott crypt," Jade said.

"Oooh, I know." Shawna waved her hand. "Maybe he was using it as a drop-off point. You know, like in the movies when the bad guys don't want the cops to know what they're doing, or in this case, moving stolen goods."

Jade picked at the label on her bottle. "Of all the theories you've given so far, that one actually makes the most sense."

For once, I had to agree. "Let's say hypothetically that Scott was the one who stole the doubloons."

"And killed Lyle," Shawna interjected.

I nodded. "Let's say his buyer, broker, or whatever they're called lives in Cumberpatch. If so, then the cemetery would be the perfect place to make a drop." Shawna wasn't the only one who watched a lot of television mysteries and knew the lingo. "Scott takes Jessica's tour, hangs out until everyone is gone, then leaves the coins inside the mausoleum to be picked up by his partner."

Grams snapped her fingers. "Only he doesn't know that Jessica stayed behind to hide chests for the hunt."

"Exactly." Excited by the progress we were making, I slapped my thighs. "Jessica hears the door creak, goes to investigate, and he…"

Shawna bounced up and down on her cushion. "Smacks her over the head with a shovel."

Jade frowned. "Geez, Shawna. It's a good thing Jessica's not here."

Shawna shrugged guiltily. "Sorry, I got carried away with the whole crime-solving thing."

"If you were right and that's what happened, then Scott and his accomplice are going to want the doubloon I found back." I ran my hand through my hair. "I say we figure out a way to let Scott know I have his coin and set a trap to catch them."

"That's not a bad idea," Jade said.

I'd been giving the idea of luring Scott and his partner out of hiding a lot of thought. "He's staying at the inn, and it wouldn't be hard to leave him a message telling him to meet me somewhere tomorrow."

Grams straightened her shoulders. "I don't like the idea of you being bait."

"I agree. Why you?" Jade asked.

I wasn't thrilled about being a target either, but I wasn't going to ask my friends to do anything I wasn't willing to do first. "Because I'm the one who found the coin." I hurried with the rest of my explanation before they could argue. "And I'm the only one who can talk to Jessica."

Disbelief sparked in Shawna's gaze. "Yeah, and…"

"And she has the ability to pop in and out. She can warn me long before Scott arrives." I didn't think Jessica had the technique of arriving and leaving a destination totally under control yet, but I wasn't going to give my friends anything more to worry about.

Jade wrinkled her nose. "It sounds pretty risky, specifically if he's the one responsible for what happened to Jessica."

"Then we set the meeting place somewhere public where we can trap him."

Once Barley realized he wasn't going to get any more scraps, he jumped off Shawna's lap to curl up next to me in the chair.

Shawna harrumphed at the cat's snub. "How about the crypt? There will be a lot of people hanging around during the treasure hunt."

"Do you think we should tell Roy or Logan, maybe get some of their guys to help?" Jade asked.

"Not unless we want them to put a stop to our plan." Which I didn't, not with Jessica's spiritual clock running out.

"If Scott's partner is a local, he'll recognize the cops right away and know it's a trap." Grams drained the last of her drink.

"Don't forget I saw Scott at the crime scene. He'll definitely be able to recognize Roy and Logan." I rubbed Barley's belly, then cringed when he sank his tiny claws into my arm.

"If Scott gets spooked, we'll never find out who he's working with," Jade said.

"If everyone agrees and we move forward with this plan, then none of us will get to participate in the hunt. We'll have to volunteer to help with the crowd." I glanced from one face to the next.

"No, seriously?" Shawna whined, and I was afraid her pout was going to last for the rest of the evening.

"We're doing this for a good cause, remember?" Jade reached behind Grams and patted Shawna's arm.

"Okay, okay." Shawna slumped back on the sofa and sighed.

After a few moments of silence, Jade tipped her bottle toward the kitchen area behind me and said, "I've been meaning to ask, what's with the mouse?"

I craned my neck to see Howard sitting on top of the refrigerator, staring at us, then back to Shawna, who I expected a major reaction from any second. I had to give her credit for the way she was handling her phobia. She'd lifted her feet off the ground but didn't scream, jump up and down on the furniture, or dash for the door.

"That's Rylee's great-great uncle Howard, and he's here to help." Grams smiled emphatically.

Thankfully, her statement didn't require an explanation. My friends had been around my family long enough to hear plenty of my grandmother's reincarnation theories. They knew better than to contradict any of her predictions or comments.

Though I wasn't about to say anything, I had to admit my grandmother might be right in this particular instance. If Howard hadn't been antagonizing Barley, then the contents from the treasure chest wouldn't have spilled onto the floor, and I might not have made the connection between the fake coins and the real doubloon I'd found in the mausoleum.

CHAPTER NINETEEN

The cool morning air was brisk, but the lightweight jacket I wore plus the exertion from unloading boxes had kept me warm.

"Here you go." Mattie leaned against the booth counter and sealed a white plastic lid on a Styrofoam cup containing the cinnamon chai latte she'd prepared for me. "On the house for all your help."

"Thanks." I clasped the warm sides and sniffed the steaming aroma, striving to calm the tension rippling along every nerve in my body. Grams had stopped by my apartment before sunrise and dragged me out of bed to help Mattie set up her booth for the Founders Day celebration.

The few hours of restless sleep I'd gotten had been filled with disjointed dreams about doubloons, tombstones, and fluttering blue wisps of smoke. Even Howard managed to make an appearance in my bizarre subconscious imaginings.

After the late night we'd had finalizing our catch-a-killer plan, I was surprised when Jade and Shawna showed up earlier than we'd discussed. Apparently, solving mysteries and stopping bad guys was a great motivator.

When it came to my friends, there were times when I never knew what to expect. I was glad to see their attire was more suited to working in a booth than going on a covert mission.

We'd decided that meeting at Mattie's booth would be less conspicuous than if we were hanging out at the graveyard hours before the treasure hunt was scheduled to start. It was also a good place to watch the crowds and see if Scott decided to show up.

Good thing, because the booths and carnival rides for the kids didn't officially open for another half hour, yet people were already starting to show up. Many of them formed a line in anticipation of purchasing some of Mattie's awesome pastries.

The first part of our plan—delivering the note—had been easily executed with Molly Jacobs's help. She was working the late-night shift at the inn and was happy to leave our message under Scott's door after I bribed her with a fifty-percent discount on her next purchase at the Mysterious Bauble. Knowing Molly, I was certain it would be something from the shop's dark and ominous section.

Jessica had also shown up, demonstrating her anticipation of the day's outcome by flitting from one spot to the next. The shimmering glow outlining her form had diminished quite a bit since the first day she'd popped into my life as a ghost.

Was the change in her appearance what happened when a ghost stayed in the living realm for a long period of time? The pressure of what my friends and I were preparing to do weighed heavily on me. If I wasn't able to help Jessica move on to the spirit realm, would she lose her glow altogether?

Shortly after her arrival, I learned that Jessica had been watching Scott the night before while we were having our planning session. She also said he'd been upset when he received our instructions, then promptly sent a text to someone. She'd tried to see who he was communicating with, but there was no name at the top of the cell's screen, only the letters BB. None of us had any idea who BB was, but he or she had replied to Scott with the message: *Stay put, I'll handle tomorrow.*

I mentally reviewed the instructions we'd sent Scott.

I found your missing item. Meet me at 1:00 pm near the place where you lost it. I'll be the person wearing a pink-and-purple hat.

It wasn't a literary masterpiece, but it was a group effort and the best our exhausted, alcohol-soaked brains could come up with at the time. The hat we'd mentioned was Shawna's idea, a frivolous purchase she'd made a week ago because it matched her hair. For now, it was tucked out of sight in her jacket pocket.

The second part of our plan involved attending the parade, then heading over to the check-in area located in the By the Bay parking lot. Since the parade route followed the main street in front of the cemetery, all the surrounding side streets would already be closed.

Serena had made arrangements with the town council to provide public transportation that minimized traffic. The only way to get there was by using one of the shuttles that either dropped off or picked up people every ten minutes.

At least we wouldn't have to deal with Lavender until later. Now that Jessica wasn't alive to supervise the treasure hunt, Lavender had gladly stepped up to take her place. With the involvement of their family's crypt, I wasn't ready to cross the Abbott sisters off the suspect list just yet and planned to keep a watchful eye on them. If one of them showed up with Scott, then I'd have the identity of his accomplice.

I was also going to be the person responsible for waiting near the crypt and confronting Scott. Not because I was braver than my friends, but because I needed Jessica's help. Her invisible pair of extra eyes would come in handy, provided she didn't get spooked and disappear when I needed her the most.

My main goal was to get a confession, one I planned to tape with a recorder I'd borrowed from my father's elaborate collection. He never went on a haunted tour without at least one listening device in case there was a supernatural visit.

If I got the information I needed, I planned to turn the recording over to Logan and Roy, then let them take over. With any luck, once the person responsible for Jessica's death admitted their evil act out loud, she'd be able to find peace. I was getting used to her ghostly visits, enjoyed having her around, but wasn't about to do anything that might keep her from moving on.

Jade and Shawna were going to find a place to hide and stay hidden until I got the information we needed or things went in a bad direction. Once Scott's partner showed up, Jade would send a text to Grams, who would then contact Roy. We figured the sheriff would be more inclined to listen to my grandmother than he would my friends and me.

After taking another long and enjoyable sip of my drink, I glanced at the other members in our group. "Is everyone clear on the plan?"

"What plan would that be?" Logan's deep voice came from behind me.

My pulse quickened, and I spun, almost dropping my drink. "Uhh," I stammered, irritated at my lack of a snappy response.

"Hello, Detective," Jade said, coming to my rescue. "We were just discussing everything we need to do for the treasure hunt this afternoon."

Shawna smiled innocently, then showed her support by standing on my other side and looping her arm through mine. "Will you be participating?"

I gave her a what-are-you-doing look at the same time I jabbed her rib with my elbow.

Logan was good at masking his reaction, but not before I caught a hint of amusement. "I'm afraid not. I'm on the job today."

"That's too bad." Shawna emphasized her flirtatious comment with a pretentious pout.

If I didn't already know my friend had no interest in Logan and had been persistently trying to push us together, I wouldn't have ignored the jealous pang in my chest.

Logan's dark amber gaze settled on me again. "Can I talk to you for a minute? Alone." He held out his hand, motioning for me to come with him.

I knew there was no way he could have figured out what my friends and I were doing, yet it didn't stop the knots from building in my stomach. I nervously glanced from Shawna to Jade, who gave me a bewildered shrug. "Sure."

As soon as I moved closer, he pressed his palm to my lower back and urged me to walk alongside him. We didn't go far, only moved to a secluded spot away from the surrounding booths and people.

"I wanted to let you know that your alibi for Ms. Jenkins's murder checks out, as does the complaint we received about your visit to her home to pick up her cat."

"Does this mean I'm no longer a suspect?" I relaxed the grip on my cup.

"That's correct, but..." He placed his hand on my arm.

"You strongly insist I let the police handle the investigation," I finished for him. "And how exactly is that going? Have you found Jessica's killer yet?"

"You know I can't share official police business with you." His devilish grin nearly had me melting on the pavement.

"How about unofficially?" I couldn't resist teasing.

He shook his head. "Enjoy the celebration."

"That's the plan."

I turned to leave and only made it a few steps when he

said, "And, Rylee…"

I stopped and cast a glance in his direction. "Yes?"

"Try to stay out of trouble."

"Working on it." I heard him chuckle as I headed toward Mattie's booth.

When I returned to the spot where I'd left my friends, I found them watching Logan disappear into the crowd.

"He is so hot." No sooner had the words left Jade's mouth than Bryce, Nate, and Myra showed up.

Bryce's and Nate's grins were a contrast to Myra's usual frown. They were all wearing jeans, and the hooded jackets not currently covering their heads were a similar dark shade. I wondered if their appearance was a coordinated club thing or a coincidence.

"We're here to help, so what's the plan?" Bryce rubbed his hands together, his eyes sparkling with excitement.

"There's no plan, and if there was, we don't need your help." Shawna took a confrontational step forward, ignoring Bryce and directing her comment at Nate.

Nate crossed his arms, held his ground, and trepidatiously returned her glare as if she might decide to pounce on him.

Bryce's smile faltered. "That's not what I heard."

"What did you hear and from whom?" I tossed my empty cup into a nearby trashcan.

"From me." Grams slipped one of the coffee shop's aprons over her head and tied it at the back of her waist.

"What?" I could feel heat rising on my cheeks as I worked through the reasons I would give my parents about why I'd strangled the oldest living relative in our family. I couldn't blame Grams for being concerned and wanting to look out for us, but a heads-up would've been nice.

"I help Mattie with her booth every year and couldn't back out on her at the last minute to make sure nothing happened to my favorite granddaughter."

I was her only granddaughter, but didn't feel like stating the obvious. "Grams, I'm going to be fine. Shawna and

Jade are going with me, and there will be plenty of people wandering around the cemetery."

"Even so." She opened a sleeve of insulated cups and filled the dispenser. "I'll feel much better knowing that you have two strapping young men looking out for you."

I knew from experience Bryce would go out of his way to do anything my grandmother asked, and it was more likely she'd convinced the two of them to be her spies.

Myra ended the discussion by pulling out her phone and threatening to swipe the screen with her thumb. "Look, you can either let us help, or I'll call the sheriff right now and tell him what you're up to."

***

By the time the shuttle reached the drop-off area, I was ready to let Shawna follow through on her threat to wipe the smug sneer off Myra's face. The day was young, and if Myra made one more snide insinuation about me being a fraud, Shawna might get her chance.

"So what's the plan?" Bryce asked once we were off the shuttle and had moved away from the other people exiting the vehicle. "Abigail said she needed our help but didn't give us any details."

I rubbed my nose to hide my grin. That was the best news I'd heard all morning. No details meant no interference. I stopped and gave Bryce, Nate, and Myra a brief explanation of everything except what Scott looked like and where we were supposed to meet him. "We'll be too noticeable if we hang out as a group, so we need to split up, to act natural."

Myra, as I'd expected, narrowed her eyes suspiciously. I ignored her and focused on Bryce since he was in charge of their group and the one I needed to convince. "Shawna and Jade will stay with me. We're supposed to be working the treasure hunt and will need to help Lavender and Serena at the check-in table."

"What do you want us to do?" Bryce jerked his thumb at Nate and Myra, acknowledging his eager compliance to my suggestion.

Having too many people involved increased the odds of something going wrong, and I didn't want anything bad to happen to Bryce and his friends. "After the parade is over, I need you to sign up for the hunt, then work your way to the security shack. Once there, you all need to find a place to hide."

"What about you guys?" Nate tucked his hands in his jacket pockets, his gaze bouncing from Shawna to me.

"We set the meeting for one thirty and plan to get there at least fifteen minutes early." I firmly believed in being as truthful as possible, but in this case, I thought it was best to fabricate the time and the true location.

"Okay, we'll see you then." Bryce motioned with his head for Nate and Myra to follow him.

Once they had joined the throngs of people headed for the main street to watch the parade, I turned to Jade and Shawna. "Ready?"

"Yep." Jade squared her shoulders and started walking with me toward the cemetery entrance.

Shawna fell into place on my other side. "I'm just curious. Why did you tell Bryce and the spoofers we were going to wait for Scott by the security shack?" She'd been watching Nate and seemed disappointed he wouldn't be meeting us later.

I slowed my pace and held up my index finger. "One, we don't need any additional interference." Or the possibility of the guys doing something heroic and getting hurt.

I held up another finger. "And two…Myra."

My friends nodded. I didn't need to explain how Myra's negativity or constant disbelief in my ability to see Jessica could jeopardize what we were planning to do.

Jade leaned closer and whispered, "Any sign of Jessica?"

She'd remained behind to watch and see if Scott met with anyone or planned to show up at the crypt. I glanced around in case I'd missed her reappearance. "Not yet."

We arrived at the check-in booth a few minutes later. Lavender was setting a stack of maps loaded with obscure clues to find chests on the counter, while Serena was standing off to the side instructing another group of volunteers. Bob had already arrived and was sitting on a chair in the corner, concentrating on his cell and rapidly tapping the lower portion of the screen with his thumbs.

Lavender looked up from what she was doing and huffed, "It's about time."

"Oh, sorry we're late." Shawna smiled, then moved to help Lavender finish setting up the counter.

Jade whispered over her shoulder, "We're not late. We're five minutes early."

I nodded. "I know." If Shawna's schmoozing kept Lavender preoccupied, I wasn't about to argue.

"Morning, Bob," I said out of courtesy, not really expecting him to respond.

Bob lifted his head, blinked a couple of times, and glanced at me over the rim of his glasses. "Hey, Rylee." Then he shifted his attention back to his phone. He was either enthralled in a game or one heck of a conversation. Not that it mattered, I'd worked with him before and knew he wasn't going to be much help.

Greg showed up a few minutes later. "Ladies."

"Morning, Greg," Jade, Shawna, and I said in unison.

He nodded at each of us in turn, then walked over to have a brief discussion with Serena. With Greg's arrival, I now had the four suspects left on my list all in one place.

Greg, who'd been late to the last meeting and had unexpectedly shown up at Jessica's crime scene. He'd been evasive when I questioned him about Lyle.

Lavender, because her resentment toward Jessica for taking over the main event for Founders Day gave her a motive for murder.

I included Serena because I'd found the doubloon in her family crypt.

And Bob because of the suspicious way he'd been acting and trying to keep me from seeing the book on expensive coins when I stopped by his store.

With the clues my friends and I had collected, we were pretty sure Scott was involved with one or more of these people. I just wasn't sure who and could only speculate on the why.

My body pulsed with anxiety, my mind wandering to the upcoming meeting that would hopefully solve two murders and help put an end to Jessica's ghostly situation. None of them acted any different than usual, and the only problem I faced now was how to determine who Scott's accomplice was.

Watching them too intently would draw attention, so I stayed busy by helping Greg hang the colorful banner announcing the treasure hunt while the rest of the group, everyone except Bob who hadn't moved from his chair, finished setting up the booth.

A half hour later, we were ready to go. Ten minutes after that, the parade must have ended, because people started arriving.

One of the first locals to approach the booth was Hank Harvey, the mechanic I'd planned to call the night Logan's truck ended up in the ditch.

Greg moved forward to greet him. "Hey, Hank, glad you could make it."

"Wouldn't miss it." Hank swiped several unruly blond strands off his forehead, the edge of his nails noticeably stained from working on engines all day. "Meant to ask, how's the car running? Any more problems?" He reached into his back pocket to retrieve a worn brown leather wallet.

"Runs great. I sure appreciate the save the other night." Greg gave him change for a twenty along with a ticket.

Greg had been telling the truth about having trouble

with his vehicle when Jessica was murdered. Hank had just confirmed his alibi, leaving Serena, Lavender, and Bob as my remaining suspects. "Here you go." I pretended not to be eavesdropping by handing a map to the middle-aged woman I was helping. "Good luck."

"Thanks, I'll need it. I'm terrible at reading these things. Just ask my husband." She smiled and gave a little wave to a man standing off to the side wearing a khaki hat and dark shades.

"I'm sure you'll do fine." I giggled as she walked away and the next person in line moved up to the counter.

The next hour passed quickly, my time occupied with taking money and handing out maps and miniature spades stamped with wording to commemorate the Founders Day event and the year. My favorite part of working the booth was answering questions for excited children.

Before long, the line was down to one or two people, and according to my watch, my friends and I had twenty minutes before our prearranged meeting with Scott. I waited until Lavender was occupied with helping one of the stragglers before turning to Serena. "We're going to go supervise the crowds, see if anyone has questions or needs help." I'd purposely phrased my words as a polite statement to keep her from assigning us to something different.

Jade and Shawna were quick to take the hint and eased out of the booth. Since I couldn't spend my time pretending to be on the phone, Jessica had done her best not to speak to me and was also making an escape.

Torn between helping another customer and answering, Serena said, "Fine," and motioned for us to go.

My friends and I, along with a large amount of dread and anxiety, bypassed the crime scene and headed to the crypt instead of trailing along to assist the treasure seekers.

CHAPTER TWENTY

The front of the Abbott mausoleum didn't appear nearly as creepy as it had the night we'd sneaked into the graveyard to investigate Jessica's murder.

"Here, you'll need this." Shawna slipped the hat out of her pocket and handed it to me. After tucking my hair behind my ears, I tugged it on my head. Since I planned to record my conversation with Scott, I retrieved the small device from my pocket.

With any luck, I'd get a killer's confession, and in case Jessica decided to poof out at the wrong moment again, I'd be able to play it back for her later. When it came to helping her move on, I wasn't taking any chances.

"He's on his way, should be here in a few minutes," Jessica announced as she appeared beside me.

It was a good thing I was gripping the recorder tightly; otherwise, when I jumped, it would have gone flying through the air. Instead of yelling in fear for the hundredth time in a matter of days, I took a deep calming breath.

A man's fishing hat adorned with silver hooks and feathered lures covered her head. It was nowhere near fashionable and currently glowed blue and hinted at getting darker.

Jade saw my reaction and giggled. "I take it Jessica just showed up?"

"Oooh, does she have an update on Scott?" Shawna asked.

"He did some texting after arriving for the celebration, but there were too many people around for me to get close enough to see what was in his message without chilling someone," Jessica said.

"She did," I reported. "He should be here shortly. And no, he didn't meet with anyone." I answered the question I knew my friends would ask next.

Shawna expressed her excitement by glancing every few seconds in the direction Scott was expected to arrive.

"Are you sure we shouldn't be calling the police for backup?" Jade asked, not sharing our friend's enthusiasm.

At the moment, I wasn't sure about a lot of things. Not only were we going to be dealing with one, possibly two killers, we were risking our lives in the process—mostly mine. "What if the only way Jessica can move on is by confronting the killer and hearing him admit to the crime?" I asked, voicing my earlier concern. "If Logan arrests Scott before we get a chance to hear him confess, she might end up being stuck here forever." And I wasn't willing to risk it.

"She does have a point, but we'll have to discuss it later, because someone is coming."

Shawna latched on to Jade's sleeve and tugged her toward the gap between the Abbott crypt and the one next to it right before I noticed a shadow moving in my periphery.

"Rylee, please be careful." Jessica gulped. "If Scott's the one…"

I didn't want to screw this up for Jessica, and I definitely didn't want to die. "I know and I will." I pressed the button to start the recorder, then stuck it in my pocket. My legs were shaking, so I pretended leaning against the wall of the mausoleum was a choice, and not because I needed the support to keep my knees from buckling.

Scott ambled toward me with the same self-assured swagger he'd possessed the last time I'd seen him. He'd replaced his friendly grin with a serious, almost maniacal glare. He stopped on the path five feet away from me and spent a few extra seconds focused on my hat. "Are you the one who sent me the note?"

"I am." I straightened my spine, trying to appear taller and project the confidence my shaky limbs lacked.

"Then you have something that belongs to me." Scott didn't have to move from his spot to be intimidating. The way he puffed out his chest and clenched his fists was working on me just fine. "I want it back."

He could demand the doubloon all he wanted, but he wasn't going to get it. I knew I'd be a liability and end up dead like Jessica the minute I showed him the coin, which was why I'd left it at the shop, locked in the top drawer of my desk. "I…"

"Wait." His gaze intensified. "I remember you." He shook his finger in my direction. "You were here the other night talking to the cops."

"And…" I drew in a deep breath, not about to let stammering become my newest form of communication. "And so were you." I stated the obvious and refrained from openly accusing him of being a murderer. I also wanted to clear Lyle's name, which meant I had to get Scott to talk about the stolen doubloons including the one I'd found. "Now that we've established how we know each other, can we get back to discussing the coin and what I want in exchange for its return?"

"Okay." He relaxed a little, then slipped his hands in his jacket pockets. "Show me the coin first."

"Do you really think I'm that stupid?" Of course he did; otherwise, his cheeks wouldn't be turning such a bright shade of red. "I don't deal with lackeys," I rushed to say before he could answer my question, then demanded, "I want to talk to the person in charge."

"What makes you think I'm working with someone else?"

I couldn't resist giving him a skeptical eye roll. "Because…"

"Rylee." Jessica flailed her arms to warn me that someone was creeping between the bordering trees to reach us.

A few seconds later, Bob crouched to keep some low-hanging branches from hitting his bald head. Speculating that someone I knew was involved with the murders was completely different from being shocked at actually having it confirmed. I remembered Jessica mentioning the text Scott received from someone with the initials BB. Was it possible the letters didn't stand for a name, but rather a shop? Perhaps Barnacle Bob's?

"Rylee." Bob acknowledged me with the tip of his head.

"Bob," I responded with a glare. There was no reason to pretend we didn't both know why we were here.

Bob glanced around as if searching for something. "What happened to Shawna and Jade?"

His question didn't surprise me. Everyone knew the three of us were closer than sisters and shared secrets. I wasn't about to let him know my friends were hiding close by. "They're off helping tourists with the treasure hunt."

"So you're here alone and they don't know anything about the doubloon you found?"

I avoided direct eye contact and nodded, too afraid that if I spoke, he'd know I was lying.

He seemed to relax a little bit, then focused on Scott. "I specifically told you in my text to stay in your room and let me take care of this." Bob's vehemence made me cringe.

An uneasy tremor skittered across my skin as I imagined all the bad ways Bob was going to take care of the situation. I was glad Shawna and Jade had done a good job of hiding. If they were sticking to the plan, now that Bob had shown up, they should have sent Grams a text so she could alert Roy.

"And I told you we can't afford to have any witnesses," Scott replied defiantly. "I already took care of the other two. The cops think the old man was responsible for the heist, so what difference is one more death going to make? With all the tourists in town for the celebration, making her death look like a mugging will be easy."

"And if you'd listened to me and followed instructions, we wouldn't be having this discussion," Bob argued.

The men faced off, and I was afraid a fight was going to break out before I got my answers. The hesitant step, although small, that I took toward Scott caused a distraction. "Are you saying you're the one who killed Lyle during the Bangor museum robbery?" The more I could get them to admit out loud for my recording, the better.

"The old man should have minded his own business and stayed in Cumberpatch," Scott said through gritted teeth.

"Shut up, you idiot," Bob snarled.

Scott jerked his head back to Bob. "I'm not the idiot, you are. He'd still be alive if you hadn't been stupid enough to leave detailed information about the heist on the computer at your store where he could find it."

"Rylee, ask them what happened to me?" Jessica pressed her cold hand against my arm, jolting me into action.

"What about Jessica?" I glared at Scott. "You killed her too, didn't you?"

Scott's features softened with a hint of regret. "I thought the cemetery was empty. I didn't know she'd be out here hiding chests for the treasure hunt. She caught me putting the doubloons in the crypt, then threatened to get the caretaker." All remorse disappeared from his face. "I had no choice but to take care of her."

I swallowed hard and tried not to shake. The only reason Scott was telling me about Lyle and Jessica's death was because he planned to kill me as well.

"My memory is still vague, but he might be telling the truth." Jessica's hat glowed, the colors reminded me of an ominous thunderstorm. I'd read somewhere that trauma caused all kinds of memory problems. Maybe when Scott smacked Jessica in the head, her ghostly form refused to remember some of the details until now.

I turned to Bob. "Why the Abbott crypt? Were Lavender and Serena also involved in stealing the coins?"

"Are you kidding me?" He crossed his arms. "Those two don't have the expertise or connections I have to run this kind of operation." His voice oozed with smugness. "I picked their mausoleum primarily because of its secluded location. No one ever comes out here, and it was easy to break the old lock and replace it with one of my own. If something ever went wrong, using their crypt was a good way to mislead the police. By the time local law enforcement was no longer suspicious of Lavender and Serena, I'd be long gone."

I wondered how Lavender would react when she found out her family's crypt had been used for criminal activity or that my friends and I were the ones who'd uncovered the information. With any luck, she'd avoid me even more, and I'd earn a reprieve from her sarcastic attitude.

"We've been here long enough." Scott pulled his hand out of his pocket along with a long red object. "I say we take the coin and leave."

I swallowed hard when he snapped his wrist, and a shiny blade sprang out. My heart nearly stopped. "Bob, we've known each other a long time. You aren't really going to let him hurt me, are you?"

"Rylee, I'm afraid Scott's right. We can't have any witnesses." He held out his palm and wiggled his fingers. "I need you to hand over the doubloon, or I can let him kill you first."

I didn't get a chance to tell them I'd left the coin at the shop, because my world broke out into all kinds of chaos.

Jessica moved in front of me as if her ghostly form

could provide a shield. Shawna and Jade rushed from the opening between the crypts, taking a protective position on either side of me. My crazy friends were each clutching a handful of rocks and started tossing them one by one at Scott's head.

"What the…? Stop!" At the same time Scott raised his arm to protect his face, Logan appeared. He rushed at Scott, taking him to the ground and knocking the knife out of his hand.

Bob took off running but didn't get very far before Shawna did another one of her ninja dives and wrestled him to the ground. Not long after that, Roy and Elliott showed up with the same young officer I'd seen working the crowd at the crime scene. They took over with Bob after helping Shawna off the ground.

I'd been too impressed watching Logan handcuff Scott's hands behind his back and yank him to his feet to notice my grandmother until she had me in a barely breathable hug. "Are you all right?"

"I'm better than fine." I grinned, pulling the recorder out of my pocket, then turning it off.

"I told you Rylee was a fake." Myra's voice filled the air seconds before she stomped around the corner of the crypt to my right with Nate and Bryce. Myra stopped in the middle of the walkway and shot a glare in my direction. "Why else would she send us to the security shack instead of telling us she'd be here?"

"Give it a rest already, Myra." Shawna stood a foot away, mimicking Myra's rigid stance.

Myra pressed her face closer to Shawna. "Or what?"

Jade stepped between them. "Or my brother will kick you out of the club." The tight smile she leveled at Bryce threatened all kinds of repercussions if he didn't agree with her.

Bryce sighed. "Sorry, Myra. In order to be a member, you have to believe." After realizing he had an audience, people who knew nothing about my ability to see Jessica, he winked at me. "And if Rylee says she can, then she can."

"But Bryce…" Myra's lower lip quivered.

He crossed his arms and shook his head.

"Geez, all right, I'll stop."

I mouthed a thank-you to Jade and Shawna, then walked over to Logan, who was handing Scott off to Elliott. "Thank you for the rescue."

"I'm glad you're all right." He frowned, his frustrated gaze holding mine. "But I thought I told you not to get involved."

"Technically, you told me to let the police handle the investigation." I grinned. "I just never agreed."

"Rylee…" He briefly closed his eyes and rubbed his forehead.

"Nice tackle, by the way." I saved him the trouble of trying to find the words for another one of his lectures. "How did you know where to find us?"

He dropped his hand. "Detective, remember? Roy also mentioned something about the women in your family being obstinate when it came to following instructions."

The phrasing seemed a little too mild for the brusque sheriff, and I raised an inquiring brow. "Roy really used the word obstinate?"

"He might have used a stronger description when he mentioned your grandmother, but I got the gist and decided to keep an eye on you anyway." Logan tipped his head at Bryce, who was standing off to the side deep in conversation with Nate and Myra. "Do I want to know what that was all about? What it is that you *can* do?"

"Uh, no." I was okay with letting Logan assume my interest in the case was to find Jessica's killer, not because her ghost was haunting me. Or had been haunting me. Things had happened so fast that I didn't recall seeing or hearing her after everyone arrived. A quick glance around the area gave me my answer.

Jessica was gone.

CHAPTER TWENTY-ONE

The Monday after Founders Day, Jessica's aunt arrived to make the funeral arrangements, and more than half the town showed up for the service. The *Swashbuckler Gazette* as well as the Bangor newspaper printed a follow-up article to the museum's coin theft. Besides providing details about Scott and Bob's doubloon-stealing operation, an entire paragraph was dedicated to exonerating Lyle and mentioning his efforts to help the police.

After everything that had happened during the past week, the last place I wanted to be was in the cemetery again. Even if I hadn't seen Jessica's ghost since she tried to protect me from Scott, I still wanted to say goodbye. Shawna, Jade, and Grams insisted they come with me.

The sun was shining, and a cool breeze swept through the morning air, spreading a floral fragrance from newly blooming flowers. I stared at the granite headstone carved with Jessica's full name and the dates of her birth and death.

Grams, always perceptive in her own way, knew I needed some time alone. She draped her arm over my shoulder and gave it a gentle squeeze. "We'll see you back at the car." She motioned for Jade and Shawna to follow her.

"Thanks, I won't be long," I said over my shoulder.

I shifted Barley in my arms, hugging him closer to my chest, then swiped at my eyes to keep a tear from trickling down my cheek. "Jessica, I don't know if you can hear me, but I wanted to say goodbye and let you know that I will take good care of Barley."

"I know you will." I heard Jessica's melodic voice seconds before she appeared in front of me.

An illustrious blue glow enveloped her form, brighter than I'd ever seen her. Her hat was gone, and her head showed no signs of the injury that had caused her death.

The air surrounding her was no longer frigid, but mild and welcoming. "I thought you moved on."

"I have, but spirits can't leave the human realm completely until all their business is finished," she said.

"But I thought once we solved your murder that you'd…you know, find peace." I didn't have the emotional strength to tackle another sinister event that involved murder or death. "So what's left that isn't finished?"

"You." She smiled.

"Me, why?" I took a step back, prepared to run if she planned to drag me into the afterlife with her. I wasn't amused by her giggle either.

Her gaze softened. "I didn't get a chance to thank you personally for everything you did for me."

"Oh." I relaxed my grip on Barley, thankful he hadn't dug his claws any deeper into my arm. "You're welcome."

"Who are you talking to?" Hearing Logan's voice startled me, and I jumped.

I turned and found him sauntering toward me. It was the first time I'd seen him wearing a T-shirt with his jeans, not dressed in his detective garb. I didn't think the guy could look any hotter if he tried. My heart continued to race, not from being scared, but because of Logan's presence.

"Nobody." I glanced back at Jessica's grave noting her spirit was gone, and certain that this time, it was for good. "Just paying my respects."

"Sure," he said, his dark eyes sparkling with skepticism as he closed the distance between us.

If he'd done some further digging and extracted more information about my family or the fact that I had a short-lived ability to talk to a ghost, he kept it to himself.

"I take it this is Barley?" He scratched behind my cat's ears, then chuckled when his wrist ended up wrapped in paws.

After freeing himself from the cat's grip, he tucked his hands in the front pockets of his jeans. "I wanted to say good-bye before I left."

"I take it you're heading back to Bangor?" I had to admit I was disappointed to hear he was leaving.

He nodded. "I'm having lunch with Roy, then heading out." His grinned. "I'd tell you to stay out of trouble while I'm gone, but we both know that's not going to happen."

While he was gone. Had I missed something? "I thought you said this was good-bye?"

"For today, but I'll be back." His eyes sparkled with mischief. "One of the men at the station decided to move to California with his girlfriend and Roy asked me if I'd like to fill in, maybe think about taking the job permanently."

The prospect of seeing Logan again set off a mass ascension of butterflies in my stomach. I used crouching to set Barley on the ground as a way of disguising the flush rising on my cheeks. "Are you interested?"

"Very," he said.

I slipped the end of the leash over my wrist, then stood to meet his inquiring gaze. A gaze accompanied by a quirked brow that left me with the impression he was no longer talking about the job. "In staying, I mean?"

"I haven't decided yet, but agreed to work for him and see how things went. I have some things back in Bangor that I need to take care of and plan to be back here in a few weeks or so."

Moving from a city to a smaller community could be an adjustment, not something that suited everyone. "Sounds like a smart decision."

"I thought so." He looked as if there was something else he wanted to say, then changed his mind. "Anyway, I need to get going."

"Okay." I held up the recorder. "Thanks again."

"No problem." I watched him stroll along the walkway, unable to stop admiring his backside and wondering not if, but when, our paths would cross again.

When he disappeared from view, I glanced down at Barley. "Are you ready to go?" After receiving a murpy meow, I scooped him up before he could scratch up more than the nearest tree. I turned toward Jessica's headstone, giving her one last silent farewell.

With any luck, I'd seen the last of the spirit seeker's magic, and there wouldn't be any more ghosts in my future.

At least that's what I hoped as I headed for the parking lot.

ABOUT THE AUTHOR

Nola Robertson is an author of paranormal and sci-fi romance, who has recently ventured into writing cozy mysteries. When she's not busy writing, she spends her time reading, gardening, and working on various DIY projects.

Raised in the Midwest, she now resides in the enchanting Southwest with her husband and three adorable cats.

Made in the USA
Middletown, DE
29 June 2020

11361992R00113